PARANORMAL COZY MYSTERY

Scripts &
Empty Crypts

TRIXIE SILVERTALE

Sittin' On A Goldmine
Productions L.L.C.

Sittin' On A Goldmine Productions, L.L.C.

pr@sittinonagoldmine.co

www.sittinonagoldmine.co

This is a work of fiction. Names, characters, places, and incidents are products of the author's imagination or are used fictitiously and are not to be construed as real. Any resemblance to actual events, locales, business establishments, organizations, or persons, living or dead, is entirely coincidental.

ISBN: 978-1-952739-67-5

Cover Design © Sittin' On A Goldmine Productions, L.L.C.

Cover design by Melony Paradise of Paradise Cover Design

Trixie Silvertale
Scripts and Empty Crypts: Paranormal Cozy Mystery : a novel / by Trixie Silvertale — 1st ed.
[1. Paranormal Cozy Mystery — Fiction. 2. Cozy Mystery —

Fiction. 3. Amateur Sleuths — Fiction. 4. Private Investigator — Fiction. 5. Wit and Humor — Fiction.] 1. Title.

CHAPTER 1

"OVER MY DEAD BODY!" My volunteer employee, Twiggy, stands near the bottom of the wrought-iron circular staircase at the back of my bookstore and shouts into Ghost-ma's shower of 3 x 5 cards.

Twiggy can neither see nor hear the ghost of my not-as-dearly-departed-as-everyone-thinks grand-mother floating above.

Thanks to my special extrasensory abilities, I have front row seats to the entire show. Myrtle Isadora, my feisty Ghost-ma, furiously scratches out messages on 3 x 5 index cards and tosses them down from the Rare Books Loft onto her oldest friend and my current bookshop manager, Twiggy.

Twiggy is shouting about not letting a certain crew into the bookshop. Taking a page from

Pyewacket's playbook, I attempt stealth mode and approach the conflagration.

As I inch my way down the self-help book aisle, I catch sight of the aforementioned furry demon spawn. Pye is crouched motionless atop a bookcase. His large golden eyes survey the battle below, and his black-tufted ears are perked. He's ready to leap into the shenanigans at a moment's notice.

Oops. Never should've looked up! I trip over a small stepstool and fall spout over handle onto my ample backside.

The battle in the bookshop abruptly ends, and Twiggy's signature cackle echoes off the tin-plated ceiling. To add to my embarrassment, Grams whooshes unnecessarily to my aid.

"Oh, sweetie! Are you okay? What happened?" She attempts to hide her smirk, but it's obvious she knows exactly what happened.

"For everyone's information, I came out of the walk-up to see what all the ruckus was about. What in the heck kind of *crew* are you two debating?"

Twiggy shoves both hands into the pockets of her faded dungarees and stomps her biker boots across the floor. Taking a power stance directly in front of me, she issues her edict. "Under no circumstances is that film crew going to be allowed inside the Bell, Book & Candle!"

"Hold on." Getting to my feet with as much

grace as I possess, which is about the same amount as a newborn giraffe, I brush myself off and square my shoulders between the two battling divas. "What film crew are we talking about?"

"You don't know?" Twiggy's cackle once again fills the space. "Hell's bells! I'm gonna step back and watch the fireworks."

She actually takes a step back and leans against the wrought-iron railing curling up the circular staircase.

My eyes lock onto the ethereal Grams. "Myrtle Isadora Johnson Linder Duncan Willamet Rogers, what have you done?"

"Oh, you know the whole story, darling. I'm sure I told you how I sold the television rights to the memoirs."

"I'm sure you did NOT. And when you say *memoirs*, you mean my life story, right?"

Grams whisks away my concerns with a wave of her shimmering wrist. "Po-tay-to. Po-tah-to. They're planning on starting principal photography this week. Twiggy is being extremely difficult, for no good reason. The crew will film all the exteriors — and something called B-roll — this week. The director wants to shoot in the bookshop. The producer just felt the authenticity of this place couldn't be duplicated on set."

Shockingly, Ghost-ma kinda knows what she's

talking about. It is called B-roll. That's all the little insert shots of objects and places that help set a scene. Her sudden knowledge of film terminology is impressive, but she's still an amateur in my book. "Seriously? As the only one of the three of us who has attended any portion of film school, I'd have to disagree. If you can build Hogwarts or Mars on a soundstage, I'm sure even a newbie in set construction could make a passable bookstore."

Grams twists one of her wedding rings and floats toward the massive chandelier suspended above the stacks.

I'm not about to let her off that easy. "Hold on, Missy, what aren't you telling me?"

"Well, sweetie, it seemed necessary to inform them that the bookshop was haunted. It adds so much to the story. Don't you think?"

Blerg. "You didn't?"

"I might have."

"Grams, you've cast yourself as the ghost in this production, haven't you?"

Twiggy stifles a cackle.

Ghost-ma attempts to shrug her designer-gown-clad shoulders, but the guilt on her face is as obvious as her missing silver Valentino slingback.

A twinge of pain in my chest interrupts my planned comeback. Playing with things I don't understand has gotten me into trouble more than once.

The torn hem of Ghost-ma's burgundy silk-and-tulle Marchesa burial gown and her missing shoe are evidence of that. But that's another story. Right now, I have to get this greased pig of a conversation under control.

"I'm calling Silas. This is a terrible idea. Twiggy is right."

Grams dives from the heights like a submarine. "The contracts are signed. We'll incur outrageous penalties if we don't make the necessary arrangements. Plus, I'll haunt both of you 'til the end of my days!"

She zips through Twiggy, giving the poor woman chill bumps up and down both arms, before phasing through a wall.

"What did she say, Mitzy? Is she going to haunt me?"

Twiggy's belligerence evaporates in the face of an angry ghost. I'm not as easily manipulated.

Shouting to the ether, I issue a warning. "Listen, Isadora, Silas Willoughby arranged for your spirit to be tethered to this bookshop after you passed. I'm quite certain, with the proper prodding, he can be motivated to cut that tether. We're going to have an adult conversation about this film crew nonsense, and no one's leaving this bookshop until we're finished."

As I wait for the ghost-tantrum to end,

Pyewacket flies through the air, up the wrought-iron circular staircase, and vanishes into the Rare Books Loft.

Whatever floats your boat, Mr. Cuddlekins.

Grams reappears from the nothingness. Her shoulders droop, and her expression is penitent. "The contracts—"

"I'm guessing you signed these contracts in my name? Since you're — let's not forget — dead."

A silent nod is all the confirmation I need.

"What exactly did you sign?"

"There were so many documents . . ." She clutches one of her many strands of pearls and attempts to play the helpless damsel.

"Look, you amassed a fortune churning through five husbands. I'm absolutely certain you know how to read a contract at least as well as your former lawyer, Mr. Willoughby. What. Did. You. Sign?"

"I signed something about life rights for the *Tansy Truth Super Sleuth Mysteries*, and—"

"Who's Tansy Truth?"

Twiggy looks at me and throws both hands in the air.

"Sorry, Twiggy. I forgot about my job as an afterlife interpreter. Grams has already signed a stack of contracts for something called the *Tansy Truth Super Sleuth Mysteries*."

This time, my volunteer employee's cackle grips

her with such intensity she's forced to bend over and support herself with one hand on the knee of her blue jeans.

"Why the heck did you call me Tansy Truth?" I have two fistfuls of my snow-white hair, and I'm seriously considering yanking out a chunk.

Grams floats down to eye level and puts such innocence in her gaze, that I'm almost taken in. "You asked me not to use your real name. I was only trying to follow your wishes. Tansy Truth is the name the publisher and I came up with when I told her we needed to change the names to protect the guilty — or whatever you said."

"I'm pretty sure I said to change the names to protect the innocent, but no need to split hairs. This, Tansy Truth, super sleuth — that's me?"

Grams dares a smile. "It's catchy, don't you think?"

"Yeah, catchy like the plague."

Twiggy still hasn't managed to get herself completely under control. Part of me can hardly blame her. Tansy Truth Super Sleuth sounds like a Saturday morning cartoon.

"All right, you signed away the life rights. Got it. What about location permits? Did you sign those?"

Grams bites her bottom lip, swallows hard, and her glimmering head nods twice.

Oh brother. "Sorry, Twiggy. I hate to break it to you, but we're contractually obligated to comply. I can see about getting you hired as a consultant so you can always be on set. And we can pack away all the books in the Rare Books—"

"I quit."

Twiggy's two words bring the world to a halt.

The color drains from my grandmother's ghost. She appears as a black-and-white phantasm. Something from a silent movie.

My heart struggles to beat in my tight chest. "Twiggy, please don't. This bookshop is so important to me. Plus, the Rare Books Loft is a critical resource for so many scholarly—" My justifications are falling on deaf ears. Time for a new tack. "How can I make this right?"

Twiggy opens her mouth, and I can tell by the set of her jaw where she's headed.

"I can't prevent them from coming here. It would cost hundreds of thousands, or more. I'd rather use that money to help our community. How can I help you make this work?"

The side of her jaw softens, and she inhales deeply. "This is how it always was with Isadora. She was the most loyal friend I've ever had, but there were risks. Isadora was impulsive. Stubborn. But always generous." Twiggy pauses and crosses her arms over her chest.

It's easy to agree with her, but I'm not sure how that will help. "What will it take?"

"You know the old Montgomery Ward department store on Main Street?"

An image of the boarded-up, run-down building flashes to mind. "Sure. What about it?"

"I want you to refurbish the place. Turn it into a roller derby arena and a public roller rink. It'll help give Main Street a facelift, and it'll give folks around here somethin' to do in the winter."

My recent obsession with roller derby makes this an easy call. "Absolutely. We have a deal. Is that it?"

She runs a hand through her short, grey pixie cut and wiggles her lips back and forth in thought. "I'm thinking about that consultant gig. I want it in writing that no one sets foot in this bookshop without me in their hip pocket."

With what little I know about Hollywood and producers, I know this one will be harder than the Main Street renovation, but I'm determined to make peace. "You got it. Deal?"

She steps forward, spits in her hand, and stretches it toward me.

My face scrunches up, and I lean away. "Are you serious right now?"

The ever-stealthy Pyewacket appears from the shadows and interrupts our negotiations.

"I recognize that look, Pye. What do you have?"

He rises on his powerful back legs, and I instinctively stretch out a hand. His dangerous fangs part, and he drops a delicate ring into my hand.

Instant flashback to the moment I opened the gift!

A silver ribbon. The perfect gold box. Inside, a delicate gold ring that cradles a cat's-eye emerald. It's breathtaking, and definitely expensive.

"Robin Pyewacket Goodfellow! Are you raiding my jewelry box now?"

"Ree-ow." Soft but condescending.

I glance heavenward, but my gaze lands on Grams.

"You know how he gets, sweetie. It might be important." Even in the afterlife, she's intent on spoiling that feline.

"Fine. Sorry for the interruption, Twiggy. Apparently, Pye thinks I'm going to land a big jewelry heist case." I shrug and shove the ring in my pocket.

Pointing to my employee's "spittled" hand, I lift both hands in a plea for mercy.

Twiggy wipes her palm on her dungarees. "Ah. You got yourself a deal, kid."

Grams claps her hands like a trained seal waiting for a fish.

"I'm hardly a trained seal, dear."

"Grams! No. Thought. Dropping!"

CHAPTER 2

HERE I SIT, manning the phones at our private investigations office all by my lonesome. It's a first for me, but it's definitely a taste of what the future will bring.

Ever since Erick announced his candidacy for sheriff, he's been spending less and less time at the PI headquarters.

In my head, I'm okay with it. Totally all right by me. In my heart — not so much. I'm a big girl. I'll get over it. Right?

Slumping against the partners desk we used to share, I sigh and mentally debate whether I should make another pot of coffee. Do I actually need caffeine, or am I simply bored?

RING. RING. RING.

My cell phone goes crazy, and I struggle to remove it from the snug back pocket of my skinny jeans.

Caller ID says Twiggy. Uh oh.

"Hey, Twiggy. What's up?"

"I'll tell you what's up, kid. Your hubby's run for sheriff is causing ripples all over my pond."

"How's that?"

A drawn-out, put-upon sigh spills out of the phone. "I called Deputy Gilbert to see if I could hire him and Johnson to run security during this blasted film shoot, and he informed me they're not available."

"Are they working on some big case? I haven't heard anything."

Another even longer sigh. "Not at all. They have plenty of time on their hands. The problem is Paulsen. She put the kibosh on all private contracts. She said if she finds out any of HER deputies are doing side work, she'll fire them on the spot."

"What in the—!"

"Since you and Erick got me into this pickle, you two better get me out."

"What are you saying? Sheriff Paulsen controls law enforcement in the entire county. Where exactly do you expect Erick and I—" The sudden realization hits me like a punch in the gut.

Twiggy's smug laugh echoes from the speaker.

"I knew you'd figure it out. They said something about crew call at 5:00 a.m. See you then."

The call ends abruptly and leaves my lips working wordlessly like a fish in the bottom of a boat, gasping for air.

Time to call my soon-to-be *former* partner — in business. We're staying married. As far as I know . . .

Dropping the phone on the desk, I hit the speaker icon and moan on about Twiggy's unrealistic expectations.

My husband's sexy chuckle eases the tension. "Look, Moon, she's right. We're a hundred percent responsible for Paulsen's crackdown. The least we can do is help Twiggy out. How long will these people be filming? A week? Ten days?"

Oh, the uninitiated. I let loose an evil villain laugh and allow him to ponder his words. "My dear, sweet Detective Too-Hot-To-Handle. This is a television series. They're going to be here for months. Do you hear me?" Pausing, I wait for his witty comeback to land. It doesn't.

"Months, Harper. And if the show does well and gets picked up for a second season, we have this invasion to look forward to every year. If you volunteer our services to run security in the Rare Books Loft for Queen Twiggy, you may as well call off your bid for sheriff. Filming days are a minimum of twelve hours. And if they pull a few strings and cook the books a little, they can easily keep folks for sixteen. We need to look into private security from somewhere. Any ideas?"

He hems and haws. "Actually, I do have an idea. Remember my buddy in Sault Ste. Marie?"

It takes a minute, but then images of our mystery dinner train ride turned into real-life murder pop into my mind. "She's the tall brunette with the K-9 officer, who I mistakenly called a *dog*, right?"

"That's the one." He snickers at the memory. "Lieutenant Juárez left the force about six months ago and opened a private security firm. She's actually hired a few of my Army buddies, plus some folks I don't know. I bet she can spare a crew. Want me to give her a call?"

The head and heart battle once again. I would definitely prefer he handle things, but a wave of jealousy washes over me. Better take the baton.

"I can take care of it. What do I say?"

His warm laughter once again touches my heart. "Look, Juárez and I are Army buddies. Occasionally fishing buddies, nothing more. The love of her life is that canine officer, Pookie. I'll give her a call and set it up. Am I allowed to give her Twiggy's info as her point of contact?"

Turnabout seems like fair play. "Definitely.

Twiggy wants control of everything. Thanks, world's best hubby."

He responds with a soft scoff. "No problem. How are things at the office?"

With a loud exhale, I lean back in my chair. "Boring! This town doesn't have enough crime."

"Hey, keep that to yourself. The last thing I need is people thinking Paulsen is responsible for a drop in the crime rate."

"Oops. Sorry, almost-Sheriff." He promises to call his friend and take care of the security detail.

Meanwhile, I get back to the important work of twiddling my thumbs.

According to Grams, the advance team from the film production should arrive today. Suppose it couldn't hurt to head back to the bookshop and see what Ghost-ma has gotten us all into?

The row of cars in front of the bookshop speaks volumes.

The first of four cars is a beat-up SUV, circa 1990s, with a pile of papers in the passenger seat and piles, plural, of empty fast food containers in the backseat. A late-model German sports car takes the next position. It has a pristine exterior and interior. Next in line, an S-Class Mercedes so new I can practically smell the telltale scent as I walk past. The final vehicle in the row looks somewhat like a dumpster on wheels. Must be one of the new cyber vehicles I've been hearing so much about.

Without tapping into any of my psychic abilities, I set a small game for myself. The SUV has to be the location scout. The Porsche is the screenwriter. The Mercedes is the director. And the strange futuristic vehicle absolutely belongs to a big-money executive producer.

Quietly entering through the side door from the alley, I hope to eavesdrop.

The first voice I hear is that of Twiggy. Her tone is unmistakable. She's putting them all in their place and letting them know who calls the shots.

A surprisingly young female voice responds.

"Honestly, I wish you would play yourself. Casting has done an amazing job, but there's absolutely no way anyone can capture — this."

Hmmmm. Too direct for a location manager. Too young for a director. As I move closer, Twiggy leads the group toward the circular staircase and begins a lecture about the Rare Books Loft.

The skinny waif with beachy-blonde locks leads the pack.

They can't be serious.

I don't even need the psychic hit that turns my mood ring into an icy circle on my left finger to know — that is the driver of the Porsche and the actress playing me. Or rather, Tansy Truth Super Sleuth.

Stepping from the shadows with more purpose than I feel, I interrupt my volunteer employee. "Twiggy, Erick's handling security."

The four guests turn, but it's the rail-thin actress who gasps and fans her hands under her pointed chin.

Rushing forward, she throws her toothpick arms around me. "My muse! Squeeee! I never would've believed you were real — but here you are! In the flesh!"

All I can think is that she knows very little about flesh, and a stiff breeze could blow her right off the set.

Grams floats above it all, soaking in the drama, and glowing like a star about to supernova. "No body shaming, dear." Her eyes sparkle.

Get out of my head, woman! Once I telepathically chastise Grams, I sputter a response to the overzealous actress. "Um. Yeah. Hi."

Rather than jumping to my rescue, Twiggy enjoys a signature cackle. "You two plan on working around the clock?"

"No, we're hiring private security. Erick knows someone."

The driver of the shiny cyber dumpster steps

forward. "Gordon Fall, executive producer and showrunner."

I make a mental "check." Grams floats just behind him, pantomiming how very impressed she is with his credentials. It's difficult to ignore.

"And this is Noah Madson." Gordon gestures to a pudgy man in his thirties, with manicured hands and sloped shoulders. "This is Noah's directorial debut. We were lucky to land an up-and-comer like him for this production." Mr. Fall motions for Noah to step forward.

Noah reaches his right hand toward me and a hint of tobacco wafts my way. Odd. His teeth are blue-white, but I suppose that's all part of the Hollywood façade. Forcing a smile I don't feel, I grip Noah's hand and shake.

His soft hand slips from mine as he says, "It's a pleasure to meet the inspiration behind these amazing stories. Even if only half of it's true, you're an incredible writer, Miss Moon. You've made the adaptation too easy."

Ghost-ma takes several floating bows and presses a hand to her ample bosom.

Yikes! I forgot our resident *ghostwriter* was conducting all of her business under my name. "Mrs. Moon. Thanks. I'll get out of your hair. I just need to update Twiggy on the security situation."

Gordon Fall inserts himself into the exchange and puffs out his spray-tanned chest in that annoying way that only entitled Hollywood producers can. "Listen, if there's any issue with security, the production will handle it. We've got great resource—"

"Look, mister." Twiggy stomps her biker boots in his direction. "You don't know the first thing about protecting this collection. She'll be handling security or the deal's off."

While I know it's an empty threat, based on the ironclad contracts Grams signed, I appreciate Twiggy finally standing up for me.

Grams shakes a fist in the air. "You tell 'em, Twiggy."

It's obvious Gordon Fall isn't familiar with strong, unyielding women. His jaw clenches. "Submit your receipts to the production accountant. We'll see that you're reimbursed."

Twiggy flicks her pixie cut back and shrugs. "Whatever floats your boat, Gordy."

Ouch. He's not a fan of nicknames. This might be a lot more fun than I imagined.

The paper doll who plans to play me in the series tugs on my arm. "Can I see your shirt? It's gotta be a great tee, right?"

She glances over her shoulder at her three cohorts. They nod in that way that people always nod at semi-famous Hollywood actors. Don't upset the talent. Rule number one.

Begrudgingly, I drop my crossed arms as she persists in befriending me.

"I'm Shawna Fenty, by the way."

Gag.

I watch her eyes scan the words on my shirt three times before she's able to process the information. At long last, "'Don't judge a book by the movie.' Fantastic."

Clearly, she doesn't get that it's a slam on her entire profession. Re-crossing my arms over my chest, I turn to Twiggy. "He'll give Juárez your information as the point of contact. You set the schedule. You tell them how to handle themselves up there. We good?"

Switching on some genuine appreciation, she replies, "You got it, kid."

The chandelier above the stacks flickers.

Our guests gasp in unison, and Shawna speaks. "Is that the ghost? Is the bookstore literally haunted?" Her desperate doe eyes are killing me.

"It's an historic building. The wiring is pretty old. Nothing to get too excited about." Then I fire off a threat to my meddling ghost. *Vanish, Isadora, or I light the couture on fire!*

Grams giggles and phases through the mezzanine, possibly into the apartment to stand guard over her designer hoard.

Before I can hightail it out of this disaster, I catch Shawna pantomiming my actions. Great. A method actress.

"Mitzy, would you mind if I shadow you for the rest of the day? It would be so lit to soak up more of your mannerisms."

"I appreciate the thought, Ms. Fenty. Tansy Truth Super Sleuth, is a fictitious character. Feel free to bring your own spin to the screen." Twisting on my solid high tops, I make a beeline for the side door before Stick Figure can ask me any additional questions.

Fun? Who am I kidding? This is going to be twice the nightmare I had imagined.

CHAPTER 3

IF I THOUGHT HEADING BACK to Harper and Moon Investigations would make my day any easier, I couldn't have been more wrong. A flash of recognition hits my grey matter when I spy the jester's hat beanie sitting atop the head of a young woman perched on our steps.

"Bristol?" I'll never forget that hat. She was a big help with the murder at the snowmobile races.

Bristol Linahan, snowmachine wunderkind, hops to her feet as her face rifles through a series of emotions. I swear, if she drops to one knee and pledges her allegiance to me, I will lose it. Better intercept.

Surging forward, I place a hand on her arm. "Come on inside. Can I get you coffee?"

Words have escaped her. She gazes adoringly at me, forcing me to continue with the idle small talk.

"How's the blog going?" Her posts about the cases I've solved are repurposed copy from the police blotter with a heavy helping of creative license. She's not officially "in the know" about my powers or Ghost-ma. "We don't have any hot cases right now. You might have to find someone else to write about."

Her arm goes slack in my hand, and, as I gaze into her dark eyes, I worry she might cry.

"Bristol, what's wrong? Are you in trouble?"

She sniffs sharply. "Like, um, I tried to get a job on the film crew. You know, like, as a production assistant or whatever. They, um, majorly shut me down."

"Oh, that's a real bummer. I don't have anything to do with the production. Do you want me to talk to Twiggy?"

She shrugs and collapses onto the sofa. I brew up a pot of coffee while she launches into her sad tale.

"Like, I heard about the series, you know?"

I've come to learn that these questions from Bristol are rhetorical. I continue to brew the coffee and avoid responding.

As predicted, she continues, "I posted about it

on my blog. The production company fired off a cease and desist. They were, like, gonna sue me and stuff."

"That's terrible. What did you do?"

"Like, I took down the story. But you know the web, bro. It's out there. People were commenting on some other posts, from, like, before, trying to get deets. I shut it down as best I could, but—"

"Hey, don't worry about it. *The Hollywood Reporter* ran an article about this production. It's not a secret anymore. You'll be fine. In fact, if they come after you, just let me know. Silas will put them in their place."

Her big brown eyes look up at me with animé-style adoration. "You'd do that for me?"

Now I know what the Grinch must've felt like when his heart grew three sizes. Powerful emotions take over, and the words come out of my mouth before I can put Jack back in his box. "Yeah. And I'd like to hire you to help out around here. Erick's heading back into law enforcement, so I could use another set of hands. Do you have time?"

And here it comes.

She's off the couch and on one knee in a heartbeat. Bristol yanks the jester's beanie off her head and bows forward. Her long braids fall across her face, and all I can hear is her solemn voice. "You can count on me, Mitzy Moon. Your biggest fan is about to become your biggest asset. I know everything about every case you've ever worked on. I can totally hold it down. Like, for reals."

It's cute that she thinks she knows everything. Approaching with a cup of coffee, I glance down. "Bristol, let's get one thing straight. If you're going to work here, you're going to need to stay on your feet. You're part of the team now. You don't need to pledge your fealty every time you see me."

She nods, but her gaze remains blank as she gets to her feet.

Handing her a cup of coffee, I motion for her to return to the sofa. "They're filming in the bookshop, you know." I suppose it can't hurt to incorporate her vernacular.

Bristol nods, and the sparkle returns to her eyes. "No doubt. No doubt. I was pretty sure that the rumor was true. It's not like you can re-create that place. It's pretty tight. You know?"

"That's what I'm told. We're organizing security for the shoot. Twiggy will be the point of contact, but there might be some things we'll need to coordinate. We'll pretty much be at her disposal for all of principal photography."

She nods, but I'm not entirely certain she understands.

"You know what principal photography is, right?"

Her bouncy tone vanishes, and she recites as though a robot has possessed her: "Principal photography denotes the phase of the film's production in which the movie is filmed."

"Correct. I didn't know you had any film knowledge."

"Noice." She seems to congratulate herself with her little twist on the pronunciation of "nice" before continuing, "When I heard about the possibility of the series, I totally got after it, you know?"

"Great. Then I won't have to catch you up. Call time is 5:00 a.m. tomorrow. Meet me at my place, and we'll step onto the set and make sure everything has been handled to Twiggy's liking. Copy?"

She slams the rest of her coffee, hops to her feet, and starts pumping my arm like a geriatric at a slot machine in Vegas. "Copy that. No doubt. No doubt."

Bristol replaces her beanie and heads for the door. Pausing, she turns toward me. "Anything I can do around here today, Mrs. Moon?"

"Yeah. You can call me Mitzy. Got it?"

Her hat comes off in a flash and she bows. "You got it. You got it."

After she leaves, I sink onto the sofa and sip my

go-go juice. These are the times that try women's souls.

PING.

Ooh! A text from my hubby. "Can I buy you lunch?"

"Hilarious. You know Gramps has me on the free burgers and fries for life plan."

"You don't want liver and onions?"

I immediately send him the vomit emoji.

He responds with the crying laughing emoji.

"Meet you there, Harper."

"10-4."

The subtle glow of the neon Myrtle's Diner sign welcomes me to my home away from home.

When I push open the door, the comforting aromas envelop me like a warm hug.

I've arrived first, so I wave to Odell and receive a shock. My grandfather isn't at the grill. It's New Guy.

He smiles and nods.

Great. No spatula salute and no extra french fries.

Blerg. I walk across the black-and-white linoleum squares to the corner booth in a huff and slide onto the red-vinyl bench seat. I had been holding out hope that Odell would never make good on his threats of retirement. So much for that fantasy.

Erick is only a minute behind, and when he walks in the door and glances toward the orders-up window. A similar series of thoughts flash across his face. Minus the extra-fry fears, of course.

He slides onto the opposite bench seat and shrugs his broad shoulders. "You think this guy will get it right?"

The silent scowl on my face should tell him everything he needs to know.

Tally approaches with two steaming mugs of black gold. "I hope you guys will give Ezra a fair shake. He might not have your grandfather's intuition, but he's a heckuva cook, and I'd love to hang onto him. If I fire another cook, I don't think anyone will work for me. Be nice?" Her thinly drawn eyebrows arch pleadingly as she bobs her head. The pencil shoved through her flame-red topknot appears to be in danger of flying free. Best thing I can do is agree before she increases the speed of her nod.

"Okey dokey."

She exhales with relief and heads off to address the four-top in the corner.

Leaning toward Detective Too-Hot-To-Handle, I whisper, "I have news."

Erick mimics my posture, glances across the table, and the corner of his pouty mouth tugs up in concern. "Is it good news?"

I shrug my shoulders and exhale loudly. "Sure. Let's go with that."

He drags his fingers through his slicked-back blond bangs and a swath falls loose. He works hard to smooth it back into place while I regale him with tales of Bristol and my big plans at the agency.

"That's great. Way to take initiative, Moon."

"Knock it off. What was I gonna do? Send her home after she lost her dream job on the Tansy Truth crew?"

His laughter comes too quickly.

"Easy, Harper."

He sighs with a "whew" under his breath. "Sorry. That name is—"

"I know, right?"

We share some light chuckles as Ezra approaches.

My inner diva is pleased to see a flicker of fear in the cook's hazel eyes.

"How's your day going, Mrs. Moon?"

"We're about to find out, Ezra."

Erick tilts his head in a way that offers me a silent, pleading "Be nice."

Taking a deep breath, I attempt to soften my expression.

New Guy places meatloaf and mashed potatoes in front of Erick, and a cheeseburger with a nice mountain of fries in front of me.

My lips curve in spite of themselves. "This looks fantastic, Ezra. Thank you."

He exhales, and his tense shoulders relax a fraction of an inch. He turns and walks back to the kitchen.

Reaching out, I rap my knuckles twice on the silver-flecked white Formica. Erick smirks. "Odell would appreciate that."

"Yeah, I think so, too." Soft silence descends as Erick and I dive into our meals. I sincerely appreciate his respect for my relationship with food. Too many people try to have a conversation once hot food has been delivered to the table. That's not how I roll. Food is meant to be eaten *while* it's hot. There will be plenty of time to talk after the hot food has been enjoyed.

As though *he's* the one who can read minds, Erick wipes the corner of his mouth and mentions, "I'll catch you up on the campaign after we finish."

Enjoying a mouthful of fries, I smile and nod.

That "smile and nod" combo immediately brings visions of my mother, Coraline Moon, to mind. She never asked me to change who I was or compromise my feelings. But she insisted unkind words were better left unspoken. She frequently reminded me if I didn't have something kind to say, I would be better off with a smile and nod.

Of course, at the tender age of eleven, my

mother was cruelly taken from me, and I landed in the too-often harsh foster system. The only way to survive was to build a hard exterior and defend myself verbally and physically whenever necessary. After nearly seven years in that environment, my tongue developed a razor-sharp edge. It wasn't until Silas Willoughby showed up at my door and disclosed a secret family and an unexpected fortune that I had the opportunity to revisit my mother's sage advice.

While it's true my grandmother had been a wealthy and influential woman, even she espouses the virtues of getting more flies with honey.

Although, it's been said: you can attract an equal amount of flies with a rotting carcass. *Comme ci, comme ça.*

Thing is, I've made mistakes, but I've come far enough in life and experienced enough hardship to know that the honey method is less likely to scar one's soul. Since I've been given the opportunity to make up for some of my misspent youth, I may as well do the best I can with what I've been given.

Long, sexy fingers wiggle in front of my face.

"Oh, did you — I was — never mind."

Erick walks his fingers across the table and turns up his palm. "Lost in one of your mind movies?"

"You guessed it. Caught me." I squeeze his hand and shrug.

His plate is clean. My plate is clean. Time for the campaign update.

Erick clears his throat. "The latest polls have me up by nineteen points."

"All right. I have two questions. 1. What polls? And B. How are you only up by nineteen points? You should be up by like a hundred points. Paulsen is the worst."

He continues to rub his thumb across the back of my hand as his eyes drift into that faraway place where I cannot follow.

"I've been distracted."

"Distracted?"

He bites his top lip and continues, "Seems like I'm leaving you in the lurch. We opened the private investigations agency together. I'm not someone to go back on my promises."

Gripping his hand with both of mine, I gaze into his deep-blue eyes. "Look, I support your decision a thousand percent. You are the sheriff this county needs. And let's not forget, I solved a heckuva lot of cases on my own. Maybe you're a little afraid of the competition."

Success.

The tension evaporates from his face, and a big grin lifts the corners of his handsome mouth.

"Maybe you're right." A sudden change blows in, and his eyes shift to the stormy grey of the ocean.

"What's wrong?"

"Well, back then I didn't know — I didn't know everything that I know now."

"You mean about my powers?"

He wags his head from side to side. "That . . . and all the other stuff. Ghosts are real. Magic is real. Sorcerers are real. Kind of shifts my entire perspective on criminals, you know?"

For some reason, that last bit makes me chuckle. The phrase is more regional than generational, but having heard it several times already today, it just gives me the giggles.

He withdraws his hand and furrows his brow. "Are you laughing at me?"

"Not even. After spending some time with Bristol today — she practically finishes every sentence with 'you know.' It struck me as funny when you used it."

He sniffs sharply. "You and Bristol, eh?"

"Yeah. She's more intelligent than I gave her credit for. And she's way ahead of me on all the tech stuff. Even in a town that tech forgot, there's occasionally the need for cyber info. Plus, she can file all the piles of paperwork at the office!"

Erick laughs. "And there it is. I knew there was an underlying reason. You better pay that girl well.

Since she has to deal with all that." He motions his hand in a circle, indicating all that is me.

Crossing my arms, I jut out my chin. "Right? How lucky is she?"

I'll never get tired of seeing that mix of shock and admiration in my husband's eyes.

CHAPTER 4

THE HIDEOUS ALARM rips me from a lovely dream memory of kissing Erick on the breathtaking Chain Bridge in Budapest. Our trip to Europe last year was filled with magnificent memories and once-in-a-lifetime moments. My bleary eyes struggle to end the alarm and make sense of the numbers on my phone.

"5:00 a.m.? What was I thinking?"

Erick rolls toward me and slips his arms around me. "How about five more minutes?"

"Are you insane, Harper? If I allow myself to be mesmerized by those baby blues, I'll never get to set. Plus, you might as well start practicing for the job you want! I'm pretty sure the county sheriff doesn't get to sleep in."

He chuckles and groans as he moves to his side

of the bed. "I'll make some coffee. What do you want for breakfast?"

"Hey, don't get up on my account. I'm gonna throw myself into some clothes, grab Bristol off the front porch — where I'm sure she's been shivering for the last thirty minutes — and roll onto the set with my eyes locked on craft services."

"Huh? Craft services?"

"I forgot you were such a newbie, Harper. Craft Services is arguably the most important department on set. They feed the crew. At all times, there's a table filled with snacks for every dietary restriction imaginable. And there's coffee . . . Loads of glorious black gold." My gaze softens as I picture the endless coffee.

His sleepy chuckle is adorable.

"You stay in bed. No need for Harper the Hero to jump into action this morning." With that, I kiss my sweet hubby before dragging my carcass from the six-hundred-thread-count Egyptian cotton sheets.

Much to my surprise, Erick tugs the covers over his head and appears to go back to sleep.

After tugging a brush through my bone-white hair, I wriggle into some skinny jeans and toss on a signature tee. Two simple lines of text: "This little light of mine • I'm gonna let it shine" above a cute animé dumpster — completely on fire.

Hurrying down the stairs with all the stealth my clumsy frame can muster, I trip only once, and catch myself on the handrail without too much fuss.

As predicted, when I open the front door, Bristol, in her jester's beanie, hops up off the step and attempts a humble bow. "I was, like, a little early, you know?"

One glance at her shivering shoulders and blue lips confirms she was more than a little early.

"Come in. Come in. We'll head over to the set to get some grub. Sound good?"

The color drains from her youthful face. "Are we allowed to touch craft services?"

"Look, stick with me. They're basically making a TV show about my life. I can do whatever I want on set. So yeah, we're allowed to pillage craft services. You down?"

"Oh, for sure. For sure." She nods her head while her smooth braids bounce in rhythm to the pom-poms on her beanie.

My sidekick and I push through the Employees Only door and merge into a world of pure imagination! Even Willy Wonka would take pause.

Electrical cables snake between the stacks, while LED light panels and diffusion filters are clamped everywhere.

As Bristol and I emerge, executive producer Gordon Fall clocks our arrival.

"Mitzy! We were hoping you'd stop by the set today. What do you think?"

"Not sure yet. I need to check in with the security detail. Anything I should know about?"

Gordon's false bravado quakes. "Can you speak with Twiggy?"

"Uh oh. Sounds like the big Hollywood producer is having negotiation issues with my feisty bookshop manager?"

He swallows with difficulty. I hadn't intended to insult his manhood, but that's clearly how he interpreted the comment. "I prefer not to push her, but we have ironclad contracts. I can easily force the issue." He puffs up his chest, hoping I'll take note of his power and status.

Instead, I chuckle and shake my head. "That won't get you very far with Twiggy. She eats ironclad contracts for breakfast, along with a scoop of Gorilla Biscuits."

My attempt at humor gets less than zero reaction from Gordon Fall. But the ethereal ghost of Isadora Duncan chuckles maniacally. "He's too big for his britches, Mitzy." She then whooshes through him, sending ghost-chill bumps up and down his arms.

He attempts to hide the shiver as he gestures toward the circular staircase. "There are two guards at the foot of the staircase and one in the Rare

Books Loft. Let me know when you clear things with this — Twiggy woman."

Yikes. Day one and we're already at a threat level DEFCON 3. After checking in with the security personnel and silently putting Grams in time-out, I head to the back room.

Peter Pan never had a shadow like Bristol. She wouldn't leave my side for all the gold in Fort Knox.

"Morning, Twiggy. How can I help?"

The dilapidated rolly chair swivels slowly, revealing a true movie-worthy villain.

Twiggy's grey pixie cut has taken on the spiky appearance of porcupine quills, and her biker boots seem extra intimidating today.

"They aren't filming in the Rare Books Loft. That's final."

"Did Grams — don't answer that! I'll see what I can do. What's your biggest concern?"

Her shoulders sag under the weight of this intrusion into our inner sanctum. "The general public doesn't know what we have up there, kid. If images get out, far and wide, it could cause some serious trouble."

"Understood. Anything else?"

She gets to her feet, stomps toe to toe with me, and whispers threateningly, "You should take out a life insurance policy on Gordon Fall. He might not make it to the end of this shoot."

Part of me knows she's absolutely kidding, but I would not want to be Gordon Fall right now. Both Grams and Twiggy have him in their crosshairs.

When I step out of the back room, Bristol is about to burst. Even someone with simply the regular five senses would be able to tell she's eager to share.

"What's cooking, Bristol?"

"Bro! I totally have a solution." Her face seems to glow.

"For?"

"The whole sketchy Rare Books Loft shoot. I can, like, broker peace, or whatevs."

"Let's hear it." I'm beyond certain she has no concept of Twiggy's willingness to blow up this entire project.

Bristol leans closer, and a familiar smell tickles my nostrils. "Hold on a sec. Do I smell Fruity Puffs?"

Her freckled cheeks twitch with nerves. "Don't worry, dude. I didn't touch Pye's stash. I got my own. It's, like, my favorite breakfast treat, you know?"

This information does not shock me. "You do you, B. What's your idea?"

"Like, let them shoot some plates of the loft and stuff. Then, drape the whole thing with green screen. And they can, like, replace the titles in post, you know?"

The elegant brilliance of her solution shocks me. "Computer-generated backgrounds from actual still shots and replacing the real titles with made up stuff *would* solve Twiggy's problem. Stick with me."

Weaving our way through members of the crew, electrical cables, lighting flags, and super-stressed production assistants, we locate Gordon Fall. I've dealt with guys like him before. Women's ideas, especially those of young women, will never be good enough for him. I have to wrap it in something more palatable.

"Hey there, we might have a solution." Always use an inclusive pronoun — to make it seem like his idea. "We'd have to take a page from your epic saga, *Titans of Ancient Egypt*." Never let it be said that Mitzy Moon skips research day. With the help of my psychic recall, I can list this guy's IMDb data faster than . . . Well, IMDb.

A smug grin plasters itself across his face as he soaks up what he perceives as my admiration. "That was a heckuva shoot. Epic. I shot that in twenty-eight days. No one's ever done that since."

I won't bother bursting his bubble with facts. "Exactly. That's how I know you'll be able to pull this off. Go ahead and shoot plates of the Rare Books Loft. Then drape the whole area in green screen, and in post you can Greek the titles. Twiggy's main issue is the value of this collection. If word gets out, we could have a real security situation on our hands. That would disrupt the shoot for an indeterminate amount of time. I know you get it." Although it sickens me, I bat my eyelashes and add a helpless shrug.

If only I had a camera rolling. His narcissistic face can barely contain the temporary swelling of his bruised ego. He hates that a woman brought this to his attention. Had I not couched Bristol's suggestion in a coating of his own brilliance, this idea never would've gotten off the ground. Thankfully, my limited on-set experience, combined with my ever-expanding psychic powers, saves the day.

Gordon Fall finally lands on a look that is an excellent facsimile of pleased. "That could work. That's how I created the Library of Alexandria. I've done it before. I'm sure I can do it again." He punches his right fist into his left palm. "We're going to have to scrap the day at this location." Mr. Fall takes a deep breath.

Without even turning away, Gordon Fall screams at the top of his lungs for his minions. "Marcus! Argelia!"

The First Assistant Director (AD) and the location manager rush to his side. They share a look of abject fear.

"I'm making some changes here. We'll need to move the shoot today."

The crewmembers swallow and seem to brace for impact.

"Get the second unit to shoot plates in the loft. Then, drape it all with green screen for tomorrow. We obviously can't get to the scenes we had planned at this location today. What else have you got?"

The First AD fails to move.

Gordon narrows his gaze and leans in. "Did I stutter, Marcus? Plates. Green screen. NOW!"

Marcus flees, yelling into his walkie-talkie as he runs.

Argelia, the petite location manager, is already on her tablet, scrolling madly. "We can shoot the crypt scene. That calls for the same actors, and we've already got permits. I can get a company to move to that location in ninety minutes. Is that a go?"

He crosses his arms and inhales sharply. "Let everyone know I made the change due to the weather. Make it happen."

"Copy that." Argelia turns and vanishes in her haste to do Gordon's bidding.

"Send me the director!" he bellows in her wake.

Argelia yelps something akin to "copy that."

The ego on this guy!

"Mr. Fall."

He glances at me, surprised I still exist. "What is it now?"

"I don't recall any case involving a crypt."

He rolls his eyes and exhales dramatically. "This is television, honey. We need an inciting incident."

My right fist is having dark thoughts. "Yeah, I get the inciting incident. But wouldn't that simply be the murder?"

Gordon Fall has no time for my questions. He shoos me away with a flick of his wrist. "You're welcome to join us at the cemetery if you need more information. I have to move an entire crew and still salvage the day's pages. Can we have this debate later?"

And by later, he clearly means never. "Absolutely. Here's to a successful shoot." I lift my empty hand in a mock toast and usher Bristol out the metal side door into the alleyway.

She removes her beanie, places it over her heart with both hands, and lowers her gaze. "You're my hero, Mrs. Moon."

"It's Mitzy. And it was your amazing idea. I just couldn't tell him—"

"Oh, no doubt. No doubt. I totally get what you did. Like, he'd never take an idea from me, you know?"

"Very perceptive, Bristol. Are you sure you aren't a bit psychic?"

Her eyelids whip open like Broadway curtains. "You think? Dang! Noice!"

Oops. Note to self. Do not joke about psychic abilities where Bristol is concerned.

CHAPTER 5

"Wanna grab some breakfast before we head over to the cemetery? There's definitely not going to be much at craft services now."

Bristol's pom-poms droop. "No crafty?"

"They're gonna be packing everything up. There's not going to be anything decent until they get set up at the new location. I don't know about you, but I can't wait that long."

She places one hand on her stomach, seems to listen to it, and grins. "Yeah, I've only got about fifteen minutes until my blood sugar goes nuclear."

As I lead the way to my Jeep, I offer a follow-up. "Hypoglycemic or diabetic?"

"My ma says the first one. But then she has a different diagnosis for me every day."

"Is your mother in the medical profession?"

Bristol climbs into the passenger side, buckles her seatbelt, and wrings her hands.

I recognize that move. "Hey, you know my story, right? Orphan, juvenile delinquent, flat-broke barista. Trust me when I tell you, there's nothing you could say to me that would either shock me or in any way change my opinion of you. This—" I gesture to the area between us. "This is a safe space. Always."

She exhales loudly. "Dude. Sweet. Mama Linahan is outta hand."

My inner child wants to scream, "At least you have a mom." But that would hardly be helpful in this bonding moment. Instead, I go with, "That's gotta be tough."

She nods her head. "Like, totally."

"Um, this unhinged mother of yours, does she have any credentials?"

"Yeah. She's a psychiatrist. She's been treating me since I was a kid, you know?"

"What? Isn't that unethical? I mean, no judgment whatsoever, but she's your mom. How can she be impartial or objective?"

"You'd, like, have to ask her." Bristol shrugs.

My psychic senses get the first hit of the day. Bristol is closing up. She's pulling back into her shell and armoring up.

Maybe I need to give a little more before she'll

trust me with her secret. "Hey, when I was in foster care, one of my foster dads was super abusive. His wife-y said it was all my fault. I was asking for it with my smart mouth. So not true! Whatever happened between you and your mom, it's not your fault. You're the child. You shouldn't have to raise the parent."

The pom-poms stop, and the tear-stained face of Bristol Linahan slowly turns. "Thanks for saying that, bro. I act tough, you know? But it's pretty weak sauce when your mom thinks you're a flunky."

"Hey, no one gets to label you, all right? You get to show me who you are through your actions. Deal?"

A broad smile lights up her face. "Totally, bro."

Parking the vehicle in front of the boarded-up Montgomery Ward, I point out the window to the name at the bottom of the faded For Sale sign. "You have any idea who Wesley French might be?"

Bristol sniffs sharply and smacks her lips together three times in rapid succession. "He's, like, a local real estate genius. Kind of a jerk, but he came from nothing, you know?"

"Boy, do I. Let's get some breakfast and then give this Wesley guy a call."

My heart soars when I see Odell working the grill today. After gesturing for Bristol to take a seat in the corner booth, I hustle into the kitchen to snuggle my grandfather.

"I thought it was over! I saw Ezra here yesterday, and I panicked. So happy to see you. We're doing—"

With the spatula, he gestures to the chorizo on the grill. "Breakfast?"

Hugging him even tighter, I kiss his scruffy cheek. "You are the best. The best — everything." Odell's gravelly chuckle follows me as I head out to join Bristol.

When I slide into the booth, I dive back into our conversation in the car. "Hey, you know what we were talking about before? Um, you should seriously consider getting your own therapist. Someone you're not related to."

She laces her fingers together and tugs at the frayed edge of one of her fingerless gloves. "I can't afford that kind of thing, you know?"

"Oh, I forgot to tell you about the benefits of working at Harper and Moon Investigations. We offer full medical, dental, and mental health care. You find a therapist that you like and trust, and your employer has got you covered."

She swallows hard and blinks back tears. "They leave a lot of stuff out of the police blotter, don't they?"

Rolling my gaze toward my approaching grandfather, I mutter, "You have no idea, Bristol." She's been gathering "facts" for her blog for years, but I guess she missed some of the humanity. Well, that and the supernatural stuff.

The arrival of my scrambled eggs, chorizo, home fries, and a bottle of Tabasco sauce strikes a comforting note.

I can't wait to see what Odell made for Bristol.

He grins at my real-life jester as he sets down a bowl of Fruity Puffs with sliced bananas and an English muffin positively dripping with grape jam.

Odell glances at me. "What's the story here?"

Forcing down a barely chewed bite, I hurry to reply. "Bristol works for the agency now. With Erick going—"

"Are you that sure he's gonna win?" My grampa scratches his high-and-tight buzz cut. "Have you got a sixth sense about it?" His coffee-brown eyes twinkle with mischief.

"Any sane person could tell Paulsen hasn't got a chance. Plus, Bristol's got all kinds of film set knowledge that will come in handy while we manage security for Twiggy on this ridiculous shoot."

The mirth in his eyes only bubbles higher. He mumbles something about Tansy Truth and raps his knuckles twice on the silver-flecked white Formica before heading back to his domain.

"Like, what's our angle out at the cemetery,

dude?" Bristol talks with her mouth full, and it only makes me adore her more.

"Eat first. Talk after."

"Noice."

We power through our respective breakfasts, and I wipe my mouth with a napkin while she slides the sleeve of her hoodie across hers.

"The first thing I want to know is what crypt they got permission to enter. You said you know my cases. Did any of them involve a crypt I've forgotten about?"

"No way, bro. Unless you consider that makeshift grave at the haunted house some kind of a crypt. This Fall guy is totally buggin'."

My thoughts immediately fly to Ryan Gosling in the big screen take on *Fall Guy,* but I keep that to myself. "All right. Then, what's his angle? How are they writing a crypt into the story? Thoughts."

Bristol tugs off her jester's beanie and stretches it between her hands. Maybe the hat impedes her thought process, or maybe the stretching of it actually helps her mental recall.

"Totally. Have to be someone who kicked it, you know?"

I chew the inside of my cheek and nod.

She continues. "Could be Cal Duncan's, right? That was your first case. If they begin at the beginning, it checks out." Bristol stretches her hat so far I fear it will shred. "Maybe they're gonna Tarantino it, bro.

Her reference to the famous filmmaker's signature style of non-linear storytelling reveals a bit more of her film knowledge. "Makes as much sense as anything else. Let's get over there and see where they're setting up."

"You got it, boss."

I could get used to this. We head out the door and, as we climb into the Jeep, she chirps, "Hey, you were gonna buzz Wesley French."

"Look at you! Earning your keep already." I grab my phone, throw it on speaker, and dial the faded number on the sign. If not for my psychically enhanced vision, I'd have no chance of reading this number at all.

Wesley answers on the first ring.

"You've reached Westie French. How can I deliver the home your heart desires?"

I've never been a fan of taglines, but that's not what gets my attention. "Did you say Westie or Wesley?"

His forced laughter grates. "Real name is Wesley, but my friends have called me Westie since before I can remember."

"Would one of those friends happen to be Erick Harper?" My mind wanders back to the story Erick told me about a friend he used to hang out with at the Rainbow's End trailer park.

Long, low whistle. "Erick Harper. I haven't heard that name in a month of Sundays. Did he send you my way? Isn't he running for sheriff again? Did you say you knew him?"

Wow. I have a rough idea of how folks must feel when I pummel them with my rapid-fire questions. In this case, I can answer all of Westie's queries in one phrase. "I'm Erick's wife, Mitzy Moon."

"Boy, oh boy. You must know all about everything. How can I help you, Mrs. Harper?"

"Close, but no cigar, Westie. It's Mrs. Moon."

"Making a note of it right now." I can actually hear a pen scraping across paper. I like a guy who means what he says.

"Well, Westie, I'm parked out front of the Montgomery Ward building and I'd like you to give me a worst-case scenario. Can we take a look at it later today?"

"You can take a look at it in five minutes, Mrs. Moon. I live over in The Pines and, as you know, that's not a far drive."

His immediacy surprises me, and I'm having trouble believing this guy grew up in Pin Cherry Harbor. I've learned a lot about small-town America since I got here, and people will rarely respond with this level of rapid efficiency. Everything has more of a laid-back, handle-it-tomorrow kinda vibe.

Bristol shows me the time on the screen of her phone and makes a gesture with her left hand.

"It's your lucky day, Westie. I have at least forty minutes before my next appointment. Let's get inside this beast."

The BING BONG of a seatbelt warning chime sounds over the phone. "I'm on my way."

Ending the call, I glance over at Bristol and she's nodding fiercely. "That guy is fire, you know? He's gonna get it done, bro."

"Do you even know why we're looking at the building, Bristol?"

"Dude, I don't question the boss. I just do what she says."

Wow. This is a far cry from the back-and-forth I'm used to with Harper. Not sure whether or not I like it.

"All right. Part of the deal I made with Twiggy yesterday involves buying this building and turning it into a fully refurbished roller rink and derby arena. If Wesley thinks we can make a go of it, Silas will handle the purchase. Can you handle the renovation? Do you know anything about construction, design, décor, or roller derby?"

With each word I rattle off, Bristol fidgets with additional energy. The second I stop speaking, her hand shoots across the Jeep and she grabs my arm. "Like, I've been studying for this my whole life. I got my AA at BCCC in architecture. And, like, my Pinterest design boards are off the charts. And, you know, ever since you went undercover with the derby team, I'm, like, next level with that. So, I got you."

I love the enthusiasm of the soul who has zero real-world experience.

"This will be your trial by fire, Bristol. Wesley is pulling in behind us now. Don't let him know how interested we are. Just because I have enough money, doesn't mean I want to throw it away."

"No doubt. No doubt. We'll keep it on the DL."

We fist bump and hop out of the car.

Westie takes one look at a twenty-something in a sassy T-shirt and a teenager in a jester's beanie and forces a friendly look to his face.

"Let's go inside, shall we, ladies?" He slips a key in the padlock, and the chain falls to the side.

The guy gets major points for his professional-ism, even though I can sense his doubt a mile away.

The inside of the store is exactly what I expected and somehow still an unbelievable surprise. Simultaneously.

A thick layer of dust coats everything. Spider webs and debris hang from the corners of the drop ceiling.

"Why is all the stuff — the inventory — still here?"

Westie doesn't miss a beat. "The landlord had to seize the property from the renters. They were more than twelve months behind, and she had given them every opportunity. Place was boarded up and secured and no one was allowed inside." He takes a dramatic pause. "Then the owner passed away and . . . Everyone kinda forgot about this place."

My moody mood ring burns a fiery circle around the ring finger of my left hand. Without looking into the smoky cabochon, I know what I will find. "Was the owner Isadora Rogers?"

He runs his tongue across his teeth and stares up at the crumbling ceiling. "Seems like a different last name. Maybe—"

I offer another option. "Duncan. Isadora Duncan?"

Westie puts a finger on the tip of his nose and points at me as though I've just solved the charade. "That's it. That's the name. How did you know that?"

"That's my grandmother, Westie. This building already belongs to me. I'll take the keys."

His entire aura sags. I'm sure commercial property in Pin Cherry sells for a decent price, and I hate to leave him hanging. "I tell you what, Wesley French. Since you're a friend of the family, if you agree to work with Bristol on the renovation, I'll pay you whatever your commission would've been on the sale. Deal?"

It's easy to see that he's struggling with the decision. He could've earned his commission simply by walking me through signing a few pieces of paper. Now he's agreeing to potentially months of working alongside a rather young woman.

"Let me sweeten the pot, Wesley. I'll make you a ten-percent owner in the roller derby arena and community rink. Passive income for life. What do you say?"

His hand shoots out and shakes mine vigorously. "Deal. You've got a deal, Mrs. Moon."

CHAPTER 6

Driving to a cemetery is a mixed bag for a psychic. Living with a ghost on the daily has brought new meaning to a place like this. Sure, I've visited my grandmother's official gravesite on previous occasions, but the fact that *she* isn't there changes things for me. What I've come to understand, from my limited exposure to a handful of earthbound ghosts, is that they get trapped at the place where their death occurred. They aren't floating around their headstones.

Regardless of the unlikely event of an otherworldly encounter, I use the technique Silas taught me for shutting down my abilities whenever I go to a place like this. While I've never experienced any visitations in the cemetery — thankfully — for someone like me, a place like this should be the equivalent of entering a high-density-living apartment.

Good news! I'm not investigating anything today.

"Mrs. — Oops, like, Mitzy, did you find out whose can they're cracking open?"

"You know how much I love dark humor, Bristol, but in this case, we need to be a little more considerate. For most people, a cemetery is a somber, sacred place. When we get on site, we'll locate that showrunner and see what he can tell us."

"Showrunner is like another name for the executive producer, right?"

"Technically, no. But in today's Hollywood, the terms have sadly become interchangeable. Although, based on what I know about Gordon Fall, he does actually play both roles on this production."

"No doubt. No doubt."

As Bristol and I make our way toward base camp, the bouncing of the pom-poms on her jester's hat sets a relaxing rhythm. Until . . .

A young girl with an expression of sheer panic on her pale face stutters into a walkie-talkie as she runs a zig-zag across the lawn.

Throwing my hand up, I offer a friendly wave. "Hey, are you a PA?"

"For the next five minutes. I'm about to get fired. I lost the groundskeeper! The mausoleum is locked! We have to get in there to shoot the opening of the crypt scene! I'm sooooo fired."

Placing a hand on her shoulder, I gaze into her eyes with as much compassion as I can muster for this circus of a television production.

"Hey, I can get the mausoleum open. Show me the way."

You'd think I offered her a million dollars. Her eyes open wide, and her rapid breathing slows. "Seriously? Follow me."

She depresses the button on her radio. "Flying in. Opening the maus."

I can't hear the snarky response because the young girl wears a headset with an earpiece. I'm simply assuming, until she verbalizes.

"OMG! They're always so rude to me. I don't know why I got into this biz."

"It's not like this forever. You do a good job on this shoot and you get bumped up the ladder. With every step up the ladder, there are more people below you. That's the dream, right?"

A hint of longing graces her features. "Yeah. That's the dream."

And that, guys and gals, is why I got *out* of the movie business. Climbing over the carcasses of my frenemies was not the path to the top I wanted to take.

We arrive at a classic-styled stone mausoleum,

complete with four marble pillars, and I give the stately-yet-compact building a once-over. A family name or motto is carved into the stone below the pediment. *AD VITAM AETERNAM*. Probably Latin, though, so that's not helping me at all. Dropping to one knee, I whip out the ever-present lock pick and tension wrench and get to work.

The lock is standard. Nothing special. But as I push the final pin above the shear line, a strange hum travels down the pick and into my hands. Immediately, all the protections I put in place vanish and I'm on high alert.

Turning to the PA, I fix her with my most fierce stare. "Tell me this mausoleum does not belong to Rory Bombay."

Her face contorts like a double-jointed acrobat. "Um. Okay. It doesn't." Her voice goes up an octave at the end.

I mumble an unrepeatable word under my breath and immediately text Erick. "Pull the security detail from the bookshop and get your fine little rear end over to the cemetery. They're cracking open the can on Rory Bombay!"

Decorum be damned. This can't be happening.

Dropping back to my knee, I turn my attention to the lock. I have every intention of re-securing Pandora's box.

Too late. Gordon Fall is on my six. That means behind me. Something I learned from Erick.

"Mrs. Moon! I'm beginning to wonder if Tansy Truth is more of a nonfiction story."

Blerg. I swallow, take a deep measured breath, and slip the tools of my trade carefully into a pocket before I turn. Then I attempt to paint my features as the portrait of innocence.

"It was already open. Seems there was a miscommunication with your crew."

His steely-blue eyes regard me. Amused and doubtful. "Works for me." He turns and bellows, "Let's get Sparky in here and light this place up. I want to be shooting in thirty minutes!"

People run in all directions, and the gaffer leads his team of electric experts inside the mausoleum to light the interior crypt.

To say I have a bad feeling about this does not begin to describe the swirling terror in the pit of my stomach.

Then it hits me. *AD VITAM AETERNAM.*

My newish ability with languages finally kicks in and I fully understand.

To Eternal Life.

Rory Bombay was not a "believer." That Latin phrase can only mean one thing—

From somewhere deep in my soul, a protective, mothering instinct kicks in. I push Bristol behind me and connect to every extrasensory perception I have, as I hold my breath.

One of the grips, the people who set up lighting gear and generally lug heavy stuff, opens the mausoleum. The heavy bronze door creaks ominously on its hinges.

Yet no apocalyptic release of demons occurs.

My psychic abilities pick up on nothing.

Nada. Bupkus.

Maybe I've created a monster where one no longer exists. Rory Bombay may have been a manipulative, power-hungry sorcerer when he was alive — but it would appear his influence did not linger beyond the grave.

Bristol steps beside me, removes her jester's hat, and bows her head.

It takes a second for me to find my voice. "Hey, what are you doing?" If she's uttering a prayer for Rory Bombay, a.k.a. Frank Freeman, I'm definitely going to put an end to it.

She gazes up at me with the huge brown eyes of a young foal. "There must've been someone who cared about him. I was just sending a little love to whoever might be sad that they cracked his— Sorry, dude. That they opened his tomb."

Bristol clearly has the opinion of someone who hasn't experienced the darkness of the world. Or maybe it's more than that. Maybe it's her choice to do better no matter what. Something I strive for . . . but not where Rory Bombay is concerned

"That's kind of you, Bristol. I don't think I want to stick around for the unveiling of the actual crypt. Let's get out of here."

Bristol grabs my arm, and there's a strange spark of knowledge in her gaze. "I know you were, like, bracing for something. Maybe it will happen when they pop the top off the crypt."

She absolutely knows more than she's saying. Now what?

Before I can formulate a clever answer, a firm hand grips my shoulder.

"What happened? What did I miss?"

The muscles tense in Erick's square jaw. His expression is drawn, almost haggard.

"Nothing. I expected all 'you know what' to break loose when they opened that door, but it was literally silent as the grave. Bristol thinks maybe something will happen when they pry the cover off the crypt, but I'm not sure I want to stick around for that."

Erick steps closer and slides a strong arm around my waist. "Please stay. If there's any indication—" He swallows hard. "We finish what we started."

Whoa. Harper the Hero is not messing around. Whatever knowledge of the afterlife and the otherworldly he possesses, he's clearly created a dangerous scenario.

"Copy that." The three of us step back to make room for the set decorators to work their magic.

When the stand-ins arrive, it makes my heart snicker to see Erick critically appraising the talent. He turns toward me and whispers, "I thought the actor would be more handsome."

Nothing I do will contain the giggle that erupts. His expression is meant to be stern, but it only makes me laugh harder as he protests. "What? You think I'm vain, don't you?"

"Harper, Carly Simon would think you're vain. I think you're simply misinformed. Those are the stand-ins, not the actual talent. These folks get paid a pittance to literally stand around while the grip and electric guys fine-tune everything and the camera department frames the shot. Wait till you see the tiny stick figure they cast to play Tansy Truth!"

The lighting guys take their final meter readings, make some adjustments, and rig up some additional diffusion silks to soften the light. Then set decorators — set dec for short — rush in with more pillar candles.

No idea why they think eternal flame pillar candles would be burning in someone's crypt, but the combination of their flicker and the light coming through the intricate stained-glass window on the back wall of the mausoleum looks super cool. Seems like this is one of those creative license moments.

The AD calls for first team on set, and I grip Erick's hand with anticipation.

Shawna Fenty struts out in — you guessed it — skinny jeans which are actually skinny, a T-shirt with a happy face on it — lame — and five-inch stilettos! And there you have it, friends: Hollywood's insistence that crime can only be solved in high heels.

The actor playing Timothy Barber, a.k.a. Erick Harper, is drop-dead gorgeous. His sheriff's uniform shirt looks ready to burst with muscle overload, and those pants . . . Oh my! It takes all the self-control I don't possess to keep from swooning. This guy would make Chris Hemsworth turn around and head back into the gym.

Erick's formerly tense jaw hangs as I lean in close. "Satisfied?"

He quickly swallows and closes his mouth. "Yeah. Sure. Whatever."

Beside me, Bristol is dumbstruck. If I wasn't so confident that her first love was me, I might feel a little jealous. Giving her a light elbow in the side, I whisper, "You should probably close your mouth."

She runs through a series of facial operations similar to Erick's before clamping her lips together.

The AD calls for quiet on the set.

They check with sound and camera, and once the director of photography says "Speed" (which means the camera is rolling), the director shouts, "Action."

CHAPTER 7

My MOTHER, Coraline Moon, always used to say, "In for a penny, in for a pound." That's my motto as we watch the first take.

TANSY TRUTH
"I know there's evidence in
Conor Mahim's crypt, Sheriff."

TANSY   TRUTH   drags   her   fingers
across   SHERIFF   TIMOTHY   BARBER'S
chest.

SHERIFF TIMOTHY BARBER
"I'm a lawman, Miss Truth. I
follow the rules."

TANSY TRUTH
"Don't be a stick in the mud,
Sexy."

TANSY TRUTH moves to the mausoleum
and bends to pick the lock.

SHERIFF TIMOTHY BARBER
"Unless you want to be
arrested for desecrating a
grave, step aside."

TANSY TRUTH
"I need that evidence!"

The SHERIFF produces a folded paper from his back pocket.

                SHERIFF TIMOTHY BARBER
        "This is a signed exhumation
        order. This is my evidence."

                  TANSY TRUTH
        "I'll make it worth your while
                 to share."

                SHERIFF TIMOTHY BARBER
        "Stand back. This is official
        business now, Miss Truth."

TANSY TRUTH smiles seductively and steps closer.

                  TANSY TRUTH
        "I'll hold your flashlight,

```
        while you open the crypt,
              Johnny Law."
```

Blerg. The dialogue is horrifying. This adaptation is way off the mark, and the lead actors have precious little in the way of chemistry.

Erick squeezes my hand and mumbles, "Doesn't seem like they have the 'it' factor, Moon."

"You're not wrong, Harper." We share a wicked snicker.

"Cut. Cut." Noah Madson hops out of his chair in the video village and strides onto the set. He lets his anger intimidate where his size is lacking.

"What part of 'inciting incident' is confusing you, Shawna? Do you think maybe you can dredge up some energy? A facsimile of fear?" He presses his hands together and pushes his fingers against his lips as he inhales. "Here's an idea. How 'bout some hesitation in your voice when you ask Timothy to crack open the crypt?" The faint waft of cigarette smoke increases with his volume.

No one bothers to answer the director during his tirade, but the moment he turns to storm off the set and return to his perch, Shawna clicks her heels across this stone walkway and plants a fist on her hip.

I gotta say, that movement is the only authentic thing she's done.

"Noah, keep in mind I popped a Xanax to keep from freaking out at the thought of seeing actual bones! When you take into consideration the effects of an anti-anxiety medication—" She throws her arms in the air. "I'm doing pretty remarkable."

The director grates his teeth together and exhales a groan.

He motions toward his AD, who calls out, "Back to one, people."

The actors return to their starting marks and prepare for "Action" to be called.

The AD shouts harshly at the sound team. "And throw a dead cat on the boom! The wind is picking up."

Erick leans in for a whisper. "It's not gonna be an actual dead cat, right?" His eyes widen with uncertainty.

"A dead cat is an extra fuzzy sleeve they pull over the boom microphone." I point to the long, thin mic suspended from an extendable pole held above the actor's heads — just out of frame. "That thing. It cuts down on the wind noise during recording."

My hubby winks. "Copy that."

They shoot the scene three more times, but to my roughly trained eye, the first take was probably the best. The effects of Shawna's medication seem to take her deeper and deeper into her flat affect. I hate to be *this* girl, but the actor playing Timothy is nothing more than a pretty face. He constantly forgets his lines — which are few — and his only expression is smoldering.

The director hops out of his chair and shouts, "Let's get the grips in here and crack this thing open. Maybe the sight of some actual human bones is what we need to get a believable performance from our precious Shawna."

Part of me is surprised to hear him talk about the lead actress with such negativity. Although, behind the scenes is always gritty.

"Hey, Ricky, I'll be right back. Gonna hit crafty and see if I can catch any gossip." I love the adorable way his shoulders slump in defeat when I use his mother's favorite pet name for him.

Bristol leans in. "Can I join the party?"

"Totes." Glancing at Erick, I shrug. "We'll be back. Keep an eye on things."

He lifts his chin and slips into recon mode as the grip team rolls in their cart.

While I grab two doughnuts, Bristol stuffs her pockets with Red Vines.

Silent as a big cat in the grasslands, a striking woman with silky black hair and gorgeous fake lashes fills a plate with carrot and celery sticks.

Apparently, I'm not a pro at hiding my shock.

She lifts a carrot stick and chomps a single bite as she smirks. "I'm Gabby, the head costumer. Are you Shawna's stand-in?" Her eyes slide to my curvy hips, and I don't need to be a psychic to read her mind.

Choosing self-deprecation, I hang my head as I reply. "Not in this lifetime. I'm the—" Suddenly, I don't know what to say. What am I? Since I have to protect Ghost-ma's true identity as the writer . . . Here goes. "I'm the author of the books. You know, the books they based this whole thing on."

She purses her full lips and scoffs. "Huh. What do you think of the casting?"

More flies with honey, I remind myself. "I was a little surprised, but I have no idea what appeals to the TV audiences."

Gabby nearly spits her carrot out as she bursts into harsh laughter. "That waif had an affair with the showrunner. Got some pillow-talk dirt on him and blackmailed her way into a lead role. Trust me, she was not the director's first choice."

"Wow. Are you sure?" The director's attitude on set makes a lot more sense now that I have the scoop.

Her expression turns inward, and she swallows hard. "Yup. Hate to be a cliché, but Gordon spilled his guts once I started, um, seeing him. I took a gig in the electric department, to get a foot in the door.

Went to fashion design school, just couldn't catch a break, so . . ."

The full impact of her confession sinks in. "Oh. And here I was thinking everything they say about Hollywood sets was an exaggeration."

We share a knowing chuckle, and she points to my high-tops. "Now those are the shoes of a private investigator." She kicks one of her Christian Louboutins in my direction and sighs. "These are the shoes of a kept woman."

"You look like you can take care of yourself — if you need to."

A spark finally flickers in her soft eyes. "Yup. I know where all the bodies are buried." She takes in my concern. "Metaphorically speaking."

"Right. Um, we better get back to set. They're about to crack—"

Bristol finds her voice. "Like, they're opening the crypt or whatevs."

Gabby sneers. "I hope they get what they deserve. I read the scenes set at Conor Mahim's crypt. If it were up to me, I wouldn't be messing around with anything connected to the actual Rory Bombay."

Raising one of my doughnuts as we exit the craft services tent, I reply, "Cheers to that."

We get back to the mausoleum just as two special tools for lifting the marble floor plate from the crypt are delivered. I still can't believe they got permission to do this, and my gut is heavy with dread.

Two of the largest male specimens on the grip crew get to work lifting the slab of stone. "Be careful not to break it, boys." Gordon Fall appears out of nowhere and supervises the opening with spray-tanned arms crossed over his chest.

The men get to work, and within fifteen minutes they're sliding back the marble slab, while the electricians switch up the lighting to get a nice hot 5K spot angled into the crypt.

And then it happens.

"Holy—" The grip nearest the doorway bumbles the special iron rod on his end of the marble slab and the stone lands with a crash.

Gordon Fall is on him like a hawk on prey. "You're fire—" and then everything falls silent.

Crewmembers gather around the open crypt and exchange shocked glances.

You know me. Patience is not my virtue. I bound up the steps and into the mausoleum. Shove aside the gaffer to get a better look.

Words cannot describe my horror.

Only a step behind me, Erick squeezes in next to me. In the blink of an eye, he grabs my hand and yanks me from the mausoleum. "Bristol, you're with us."

In less than thirty seconds, he's placed Bristol

and me firmly in my Jeep. Now he's insisting we go directly to Silas Willoughby.

"Erick, Bristol can't—"

He exhales in frustration. "Hey, if she's going to work for you, she needs to know the whole story. Fill her in on the drive. I've got to talk to Paulsen. Would you rather do that?"

The thought of confronting Sheriff Paulsen with sketchy information about Rory Bombay's empty crypt is definitely not something I want to do.

"Fine, you win. I'll be at Willoughby's. Stop by the bookshop and update Twiggy and Grams. And get that security detail back in there. We have absolutely no idea how this is going to play out."

He takes one look at me, and the set of his jaw worries me almost more than the empty crypt.

"If memory serves, Moon, we know exactly how this is going to play out. You were always his target. This time, I'm going to be a step ahead. Get to Willoughby's."

As I drive out of the cemetery with reckless abandon, memories of my last fateful encounter with Bombay come flooding back. The thing that concerns me most is the current tingling in the palm of my right hand.

Gulp.

I remember this same feeling when I held that

enchanted ring for a quick second before I slipped it into my pocket. At the time, Silas had warned me that removing the ring from Rory's lifeless hand could come back to haunt me, but there was no way I could let something that powerful follow him to the grave.

Now we find out if I made a good choice or a bad choice.

CHAPTER 8

OUR DRIVE TAKES US to the edge of town in silence before Bristol's innate curiosity gets the best of her.

"What'd Erick mean by 'the whole story', bro?"

On cue, every fiber of my being screams NO. Don't tell anyone your secrets. If she knows the truth about you, she'll think you're a freak! All the old foster-care fears bubble to the surface in an instant.

Bristol tugs off her jester's beanie, places it in her lap, and folds her hands on top of it. Her silence seems to fill the car.

Here goes nothing. Inhaling sharply, I launch into my story. "You know the clues and stuff — that you write about on your blog?"

She bobs her head, and her braids twitch back

and forth. "Yeah. Totes. You're, like, fire at solving crimes, you know?"

"Yeah. Thanks." My mouth goes dry, and I can scarcely force myself to swallow. "I have kind of a special advantage." Breathe. "I'm a psychic."

Brace for impact.

Bristol turns, and her gaze is unreadable. "Yeah, like, totally."

"What do you mean? Like, totally?"

"Oh, for sure. Like, I totally know that. That's why you're so awesome."

I'm not sure whether to be relieved that she didn't flip out or offended that she assumed I couldn't solve crimes with the normal five senses.

"There's more to it, all right? I have other powers." Suddenly, I feel as though I have something to prove.

Again, her head bobs in agreement. "No doubt. No doubt."

"And you're cool with it?"

She picks at her dry cuticle and gives my question a moment of consideration. "Oh, for sure. For sure."

"All right then. Buckle up, Bristol. You're about to get a drink from a fire hose."

She straightens her shoulders and appears ready for anything.

"Right now, we're driving to Silas Willoughby's

house. You probably know him as my lawyer. He was my grandmother's lawyer before mine." I wait for some sign she agrees, and continue, "He's more than that. I mean, the minute you see his house, you'll probably get it. Silas has a ton of arcane knowledge. He owns piles of interesting artifacts, and he's kind of my mentor. He helps me figure out my powers."

She sniffs sharply. "No doubt. No doubt."

It's bugging me that she's so completely unflappable. Might as well drop the ghost bomb and see how that affects her intense calm.

"And my grandmother's ghost lives in the bookshop. Like I can see her and talk to her." Not sure why I'm getting so defensive.

"Noice." A huge smile breaks across Bristol's freckled face, and she nods to a rhythm that exists only in her head.

"Seriously? You're not freaked out by the psychic thing? The powers? Or even ghosts living in my bookshop?"

"No way, dude. It's epic. I'm all in. For all of it. I got your back, Mrs. — Mitzy."

"Wow. I can't believe you're so cool with everything. I wish there were more people like you in the world."

Bristol twists one of her braids around her finger as she nods. "You might be shook, dude.

Maybe, like, you need to let more people in, you know?"

Yikes! Who knew I was going to be hit with the wisdom of a Gen Z philosopher? "Thanks for saying that. You know some of my back story, yeah?"

She nods.

"So, with the foster care stuff . . . I kind of have trouble trusting people." I swallow hard and exhale.

Bristol continues to bob her head. "I get it, dude. Finding out I was adopted messed me up at first too, but, like, we're just a collection of all our experiences, you know? You decide how to run your life now. Right?"

That one sounds like it needs an answer. "Right. I'm definitely going to enjoy working with you, Bristol. Hiring you might be the best thing I've done since I stepped off that sketchy bus and landed in Pin Cherry Harbor."

She bursts into outright laughter. "No way! Bagging Detective-Too-Hot-To-Handle was the killer move, dude."

We share a wicked chuckle. "You're right. Erick is kinda my one in a million."

She shakes her head. "No way. He's your one-and-done. That's for life right there, bro."

"Yeah, it is."

Turning down Mr. Willoughby's drive always

brings a sense of wonder. The black-and-white bark of the birch trees flashes past, and late October light penetrates the turning leaves, creating a mysterious yet welcoming glow.

As the dwelling in the forest looms into view, its perfect eccentricity enchants me. An awe-inspiring Gothic structure with three haunting stories and small dormers in the roof, showing evidence of a usable attic space. Sharply pointed turrets accent the corners, and intricate stained-glass windows catch the angled sun. The home is not in disrepair, but it has clearly waged a lengthy battle with time and has given up a little ground with each passing year.

When I take the secret turn, Bristol gasps. She grabs the oh-no handle above her head. "What the—"

"Oh, it's a turn that only certain people can see. Sorry. I forgot to warn you."

She lets go of the handle and slips her beanie off in reverence. "Dude. Sweet."

Erick must've called Silas, after he updated Grams and Pyewacket at the bookshop. My mentor stands on the stone steps beside his three-car carriage house. His fusty tweed coat appears to have a new indigo stain near the hemline. The results of some special alchemical solution leaking from one of his many hidden pockets, no doubt. He smooths his bushy grey mustache with a thumb and fore-finger as he waits for me to park.

When I step out of the vehicle, he makes a ges-ture in the air, and Bristol stops in her tracks like a robot with a dead battery.

"Mizithra Achelois Moon, why would you bring an outsider to my property?"

Yikes. Formal name territory, *and* he's openly practicing alchemy. Assuming that's what hap-pened to Bristol.

"Didn't Erick call you?"

"I received a brief telephone call from your hus-band, indicating a potential disaster in play. He no-tified me you were en route. I was not informed of a guest."

"It's all right. This is Bristol Linahan. I hired her to help me at the agency and — she knows every-thing, Silas. Can we just go into the house so I can tell you about this whole Rory Bombay debacle?"

His thick eyebrows squirm like caterpillars moving to higher ground, and the milky film that normally covers his eyes vanishes. Sharp blue eyes knife into me. "Come inside at once." He draws three symbols in the air, and Bristol continues walking as though nothing happened.

Compared to her reaction to my "I see dead people" reveal, Bristol's entire vibe shifts once she enters the home of Silas Willoughby. My new assistant's jaw hangs slack, and her head swivels on her neck like one of those bobble dolls on a dashboard. She can't seem to take it all in fast enough.

We finally arrive in the library, where the polished marble floor boasts an impressive collection of hand-knotted rugs. The standard pile of ancient tomes seems to test the strength of the sturdy oak table in the center of the curved room. The arcane collection in this room definitely rivals the Rare Books Loft.

My eyes dart toward the great toe of the life-sized marble statue of Hermes Trismegistus. On my last visit to this special room, Silas revealed the toe's importance as the first step to opening his otherwise impenetrable vault. I wonder if Silas still has Rory's cursed ring in his vault?

Unlike the gorgeous emerald ring Pyewacket retrieved earlier, also a gift from Rory — that cat knows everything — the ring I removed from Rory Bombay's lifeless hand had a curse that could not be removed.

Mr. Bombay had enchanted the ring to both peer into the minds of others and attempt to control their actions. Thanks to my mentor's training, I had mostly resisted the ring's power. A dangerous weapon like that had to be kept from the wrong hands. The vault of Mr. Silas Willoughby is the safest place that I know of on earth.

"Mizithra, I have scant information on the events which took place at the cemetery. Your husband was dead set on what he called 'getting a jump' on the situation. Please regale me with every detail of this morning's misadventure."

After laying the necessary groundwork with what we call in the biz "backstory," I share the big reveal with Silas.

"As soon as we saw the crypt was empty, Erick escorted me out of there, and that's all I know."

Silas paces in silence. Occasionally he pauses, and his arthritic finger glides down the spine of some mystical volume.

Bristol's patience finally wears thin. She sidles next to me and whispers, "Is he always like this?"

Leaning toward her, I murmur, "Most definitely." She slips off her hat and pulls at some loose threads on one of the pom-poms. I only hope that she doesn't somehow unravel the hat and drop yarn shreddings all over my mentor's sacred library.

Fortunately for both of us, he finishes the final lap and stops before us. "I can say with a high degree of certitude that Mr. Bombay did not cheat death. I've only ever known one item with the power of resurrection." His sharp eyes lock onto mine. "And we both know that artifact no longer exists."

His reference to the Oracle of Return and its use, in my hands, hits home.

"Well, what do you think happened to Rory's remains? Could he be a zombie?"

For some reason, this assertion tickles my mentor's funny bone. His laughter reddens his cheeks and jiggles his jowls. "Your generation and their obsession with zombies. Once again, I do not believe that to be the case."

Bristol has reached her limit. "So, like, what happened to the dude?"

It amuses me to watch Mr. Willoughby's features twist to and fro as he attempts to decipher this new language. "My first and best guess would be good old-fashioned grave robbers."

"Silas, you can't be serious." My eyes roll of their own free will. "People don't rob graves in this day and age. Unless — Do you think he would have been buried with some important artifacts? In that case—"

Beside me, Bristol blurts, "That chick! That chick at that antique place. She'd know the skinny, right?"

Silas gazes at her in near horror. However, I pick up what she's laying down. That "chick" is likely our best hope of getting information.

"Silas, whatever happened to Bombay Antiquities and Artifacts in Grand Falls? I kind of assumed it would be boarded up after its owner passed away. Do you think that Southern belle lady is still running the place?"

Bristol's fingers are already flying across the screen of her phone. "Nope. Place closed. Like, six months after Bombay kicked it."

Silas tilts his head like a confused puppy and glances at me for help.

"She's saying that the antique store went out of business a few months after Rory's passing."

He harrumphs and smooths his mustache. "Perhaps. I believe this hypothesis deserves proof. This calls for a small road trip, ladies."

Silas leads the way toward his garage. My heart drops. The last thing I want to do in late October, in almost-Canada, is hop into a 1908 Model T. I don't care how mint its condition.

"I'll drive, Silas. Do you need to bring . . . anything?"

I hope my meaningful stare carries the correct amount of *hint*.

Silas pats down his stained tweed coat and shakes his head. "I believe I have all that I require."

With that, the three of us load into my Jeep and head toward Grand Falls, hoping to find a boarded-up antique store and no Zombie Bombay.

CHAPTER 9

THE COLORFUL AUTUMN leaves provide a picturesque drive to Grand Falls, while my mentor turns the journey into a private tour. Silas Willoughby seems to have lived in the area since long before the steam engine or electricity made their debuts. Despite his dated lingo, the information holds our interest, and, most importantly, takes our minds off the looming specter of Rory Bombay.

"This scenic route around Lake Dimii, the Ojibwe word for deep water, was the original north-south wagon train route. It was eventually adopted by early Pony Express riders, and on the heels of the invention of motorized vehicles became a vital trade thoroughfare. It was added to the state's official highway map and given the designation 169 in 1933."

Bristol dares a question. "Did that Pony Express place sell stamps and, like, packing materials?"

Silas swivels his torso to ensure she receives the full measure of his horrified stare. "My dear girl, in what year were you born?"

She leans forward and smirks. "2006, baby. That was the last good year, you know?"

Silas, recognizing when he's been beat, returns his gaze forward and mumbles, "I was not aware."

Gotta smooth things over. "When was the city of Grand Falls established?" The fastest way to get us back on track is to get Willoughby talking.

He takes the bait. "Grand Falls was the first county seat in Lake County."

Now it's my turn to interrupt. "Wait. What? Grand Falls isn't in Birch County?"

"Indeed, it is not. We passed through the southern border of Birch County approximately twelve minutes ago."

"Wow. I had no idea."

Silas turns and beams with fatherly pride. "Now you understand why your efforts were so critical in unraveling Walter Johnson's homicide. You were able to skip the delays that come with inter-agency cooperation."

My mentor's throwback to my second case sends me spiraling down memory lane. That solemn look on Odell's face when he asked for my help in figuring out what happened to his younger brother. It was a terrifying case, because of all the trouble I got into, but that shouldn't surprise any of you. The nice part was, I made a lifelong friend in Walt's daughter, Diane. Especially when I later discovered my genetic connection to Odell. I finally had a cousin. Kind of exciting — for an orphan.

Silas reaches over the console and pats my shoulder. "I did not intend to bring upsetting memories to the surface."

"It's not upsetting. Not now. It's kinda comforting to look back and see how far I've come. How far *we've* come. That was when you first taught me to remove handcuffs without a lock pick." A sudden wave of emotion hits me. "It was also the first time you sacrificed yourself to save me."

His milky-blue eyes fill with emotion, and I know he's thinking about those we've lost along the way. Those we couldn't save.

He gives my shoulder a final squeeze and nods once in silence.

Bristol, eager to be part of the inner circle, pushes herself between the seats and rests her elbows on the console. "Mr. Willoughby, can you teach me that stuff? Getting outta handcuffs and other, you know, sweet tricks?"

Blerg. If only she hadn't said sweet tricks. It's

too late for me to walk it back. She'll have to learn her lessons the hard way. Just like I did.

"Ms. Linahan, your eager determination has merit. However, when dealing with the alchemical world, nothing can be rushed. Skills begin at the simplest of levels, and each small brick of knowledge builds on those beneath. Alchemy is a lifelong practice. It is not, nor has it ever been, a series of sweet tricks."

Silas never turns his head, but the effect of his words is evident in Bristol's withdrawal. She seems to fold in on herself like collapsing origami as she retreats into the back seat in silence.

I feel for the kid. "Hey, there's the antiquities place. It's definitely been boarded up. Should I pull around back and see if there's any evidence of recent access?"

"An excellent idea, Mizithra."

Sounds like I better tread lightly. Once you've offended his alchemical senses, it takes a good deal of prostration to get back into his good graces.

Turning into the alley behind the shop, I park close to the door, using the vehicle to hide my activities. It seems like a marginally abandoned part of town, but I can't risk drawing the attention of law enforcement in a county where I have no pull.

As I hop out of the vehicle, Bristol joins me. "I'll

hoof it to the corner and call if I see anything. One ring and I'll hang up."

Glancing at my new sidekick and certainly former juvenile delinquent, I grin. "Excellent point, Number Two."

Her face is blank, but that doesn't stop her from turning and running toward the corner.

Note to self: work on Bristol's film knowledge. I can't be tossing my callbacks into an info void. I need them to land every once in a while. If for no other reason than my fragile ego.

Silas rolls down the passenger window and speaks softly. "Perhaps a cloak of invisibility would be in order."

I find it adorable that he has no idea he's referencing an incredibly popular fandom. Offering him a hearty thumbs-up, I calmly center myself and take three deep breaths.

Fairly certain I've achieved invisibility, for the time being, I crouch beside the lock and quickly gain access.

"Mizithra. Halt."

That's not a tone of voice that allows for questions. Rather than pushing open the door, I freeze where I'm at as my mentor joins me. Silas places a flat palm on the door, removes it, and retrieves a tiny blue vial from one of the inner pockets of his coat.

He loosens the cap, pours the mixture into his left hand, and blows. A sparkly cloud takes flight and coats the door.

He touches my shoulder and utters a single word, "Now."

Pushing open the door, I hold it as Mr. Willoughby joins me.

"Was there some kind of spell? I didn't sense anything."

He shakes his head, making his jowls jiggle. "Nothing so exciting. Simply a mundane security system. That alchemical working will give us a maximum of fifteen minutes. Search quickly and purposefully."

Heading straight for the desk where I discovered an item of great power on my last visit, I'm disappointed to see the back room nearly empty. The few shelving units that remain are devoid of inventory.

Silas harrumphs. "I believe the woman who managed this place for Mr. Bombay must have evacuated with remarkable speed upon learning of his death."

In an effort to stave off any resurfacing visions, I hustle to change the subject. "We have to find her. She's the only person I know who had any connection to him. If she did take everything and skedaddle, like you think, she had to go somewhere.

Should we go to the PI's office or back to your place?"

Without answering, he grips my shoulder and tugs me toward the rear entrance. "The working did not have the strength I expected. We must leave at once."

As the door closes behind, a loud alarm bell rings.

Slamming the accelerator to the floor, I flip a tight U-turn and barely slow down long enough to allow Bristol to leap into the backseat.

Silas directs me, and I follow with the intense focus of a rally car driver.

Once we've put four or five blocks between the former antiquities storefront and us, he places a calming hand on my knee. "Please return to the legal speed limit and aim this beast of a vehicle toward home."

I lift my foot off the gas pedal, take a deep breath, and attempt to look as though everything is normal.

"Would that be my home or your home, Silas?"

He smooths his bushy mustache with a thumb and forefinger. "I believe it is time we explore the domain of Ms. Linahan. The information we seek may be most aptly acquired at her fingertips."

Bristol nearly explodes with delight. "Noice." She gives me her address, and I shake my head.

"That means nothing to me. Just tell me where to turn. I know my way back to Pin Cherry. But, you know, when we get close."

"No doubt. No doubt."

If I correctly interpreted my mentor's command, he's actually counting on Bristol's tech skills. This will be a Harper and Moon first.

SINCE WE HIT THE EDGE OF TOWN, Bristol has been unstoppable. She's giving directions, filling in her backstory, and fruitlessly attempting to ingratiate herself with Silas.

When she signals the last turn, my eyes want to eject themselves from my skull. "Rainbow's End? You live in Rainbow's End? Is that why you knew so much about Westie?"

She points at a bright-teal trailer on the right with an enormous sign on its front lawn. "Birthplace of Wesley French. The number one realtor in Birch County."

The sign is as faded as the accolade. The year, 2016, hangs onto the corner with the last bits of its red paint. I suppose there aren't many things to celebrate in this trailer park. Good for them. They have that.

Bristol points to a grey trailer on the left with a sagging roof partially covered by a large swath of blue plastic held down by three old tires and two bricks.

Forcing myself to shove the heiress back into her golden box, I look at the trailer through the eyes of a broke barista, scraping by paycheck to paycheck.

"You have your own place? Good for you."

She beams with pride. "Yeah, I worked my a—Sorry. I worked super hard while I was going to school to save all my Benjamins, you know?"

"Yeah. Totally. Do you have any roommates?"

"Nah. Not anymore. AJ and Crank used to live here. But, you know, I, like, outgrew them."

There's potentially an entire sordid tale behind that one sentence, but now is not the time to head down bad-memory lane. Whatever happened between her and her former snowmachine racing buddies is a tale for another time.

"After I drop you and Silas off, I can run get snacks or whatever you want." I don't want to ask outright if she has food.

"Don't worry about it, bro. I'm loaded for snacks. Like, loaded."

"Sweet." This should be interesting.

Silas, as though reading my mind, offers his query. "May I be so bold as to inquire whether you have tea, Ms. Linahan?"

"Totes. I got, like, this sampler, you know? All

kinds of stuff. I can boil up some water for you in no time."

Well, there goes my chance of escaping any part of this questionable experience. I turn off the engine, and we unload and head up the wooden steps to her surprisingly sturdy porch. She slips the key in the first lock and calls over her shoulder, "You better lock the rig. Some people around here are super sketchy, you know?"

"Oh, I know." Clicking the fob, I lock my Jeep and wait for Bristol to open the remaining two locks on her front door.

The three of us enter, and I force myself to remain nonreactive.

The barren living room contains a beanbag chair slouched atop grey-green carpet, some kind of gaming system, and a shockingly large television screen. The kitchen houses one compact, square table and two well-worn chairs.

As I glance briefly down the hallway, two doors are visible on the left, and there's a room at the end. Hmmm, potentially two bedrooms and one bath. The entire place is clean, except for the pile of dishes in the sink.

She catches my line of sight and stutters, "Like, I was upset about not getting that crew job. I can totally wash the dishes before we get started."

Silas lifts a hand to swish away her concerns.

"We are not here to pass judgment on your lovely home, Ms. Linahan. I require your technical expertise in accessing any records associated with Rory Bombay, a.k.a. Frank Freeman, and his various enterprises."

Bristol whips off her beanie, loosens up her fingers, and grins. "At your service, bro."

CHAPTER 10
ERICK

MY WIFE IS A FORCE OF NATURE. I never expect her to check in, or be at my beck and call, but right now, I absolutely need her to answer her phone. "Moon, pick up. Pick up!"

"Hey, almost-Sheriff. What's up?"

"Gilbert Murray was electrocuted."

"Deputy Gilbert?"

"No. Not the deputy. This guy's *first* name is Gilbert. This guy, Gilbert Murray, is something called a gaffer on—"

"What? Not even! A guy who actually knows everything there is to know about electricity is electrocuted on set? There's no way that's an accident."

I exhale a few drops of tension. "That's exactly what I thought. I know I whisked you away from the cemetery with no discussion, Moon. Sorry about that. I kinda let fear control me. Maybe you need to get back over here and see if there's some vengeful spirit attacking the crew."

She emits a steady hum, and I can almost see her soft-grey eyes rolling back and forth as she thinks.

"I'm out at Bristol's place, with Silas. We're looking into Rory's financials and corporate records. The antiquities place in Grand Falls was totally cleared out. We need to find that woman, that southern-talking woman, who ran the place for Bombay."

"Opal Williams?"

"Are you serious right now, Harper?"

"Sure. I might've seen the name on some of the Walt Johnson homicide paperwork. Seems like Walt sold a bunch of stuff to Gershon's Antiques before Rory bought the place. Could be wrong."

Mitzy exhales a low moan and replies, "Not likely. I'm starting to think you're some kind of psychic savant, Harper."

Her sense of humor always lightens the mood. "I'm headed to the hospital to see if Murray can make a statement. What's your next move?"

Mitzy's breath catches. "The gaffer is still alive?"

"Yeah. According to the witnesses here — a grip is what he called himself — he grabbed a wooden broomstick and pried Murray off the genny. I don't know what a genny is, but the accident happened by the mobile electric generator, so I can warrant a guess."

"Maybe it was a legitimate accident. Accidents do happen."

As much as I love my wife and frequently take her left-field suggestions, this one does not sit right with me.

"No way, Moon. Your instincts have to be right. There's no way a guy who's been in the industry for over fifteen years and worked his way up to the top position in the electrical department made this mistake. It's gotta be Bombay's ghost."

"I hope you're not right." A soft groan escapes as Mitzy continues, "Silas will have his hands full for a while. I'll head back to the cemetery and have a snoop."

The thought of her coming here after I leave, to face a possibly dangerous ghost—

"Meet me here. I can go to the hospital later. Murray is probably in no condition to talk to me anyway."

"Harper, I can take care of myself. I appreciate your concern, but I'm a lot stronger now. I got this. You get to the hospital and find out everything you can. You need to contact him before anyone else. If it wasn't an accident or a ghost, Murray will be in danger."

I hate to admit she's right. "10-4. Can you at least report in every half hour — on the dot?"

Her easy laughter scrubs away a layer of my concern. "You got it, Sheriff. Honorary Deputy Moon checking in every half hour. 10-4. Over and out."

That woman will seriously be the death of me.

Distraction is my go-to coping mechanism. Revving the engine as I peel out of the cemetery parking lot pushes away the gloom, for a minute.

Racing toward the Birch County Regional Medical Center, I run through various scenarios. She could be right. Accidents do happen. Things were moving fast on that set. Maybe somebody just screwed up.

The emergency sign pushes into view, and I throw a hard right into the parking lot.

Over the years, I made a lot of friends and allies here. I never rubbed my badge in anyone's face and never spent longer than they told me with recovering patients. I figured if I respected their jobs, they'd respect mine.

Now we find out if any of that goodwill still carries weight around here.

Entering through the automatic double doors at

the emergency bay, I lift my chin and walk directly to the check-in desk.

A familiar face, probably someone who attended high school with me, looks up with a grin. "Sheriff Harper. Are you injured?"

The name thankfully pops into my head. "Wrong on both counts, Amanda. I'm not the sheriff right now. Just campaigning. And I'm not injured. I'm actually here about Gilbert Murray. We're working security for the production company, and I need to get a statement from him as soon as possible."

She hops to her feet with a concerned but cheerful expression. "Absolutely. He just came around about ten minutes ago. Follow me."

Amanda walks toward her side of the secure door between the lobby and the emergency treatment area, and I wait for her to buzz me in.

"Thanks."

"No problem, Erick."

As she leads the way toward his bed, she looks over her shoulder. "You got my vote, dontcha know."

"Thanks, Amanda. Every vote counts."

Despite knowing I'm a better sheriff than Paulsen, it's never easy to unseat an incumbent. She may be riding on the crest of a wave I put in motion, but the low crime rate is something residents won't ignore.

"Here we are. I'd say you have about fifteen minutes before the attending makes his rounds." She winks and heads back to her desk.

Happy to know that my goodwill still opens a few doors.

The man in the bed is hooked up to an IV, pulse ox monitor, EKG, and there's an oxygen tube in his nose. Good, he can still talk.

"Mr. Murray, I'm Erick Harper. With the security company working for the production. Do you feel okay? Can you tell me what happened?"

His eyes roll toward me, and there's zero acknowledgment.

Pulling up a chair, I sit near his bed and try a softer approach. Patting his hand, I tell him what I know, and use the word "accident" as many times as I dare.

His vision seems to steady, and his pale-green eyes focus on my face.

"No accident."

"I'm honestly glad to hear you say that. Couldn't imagine anyone with your experience and years on set making a mistake like that. Walk me through what happened."

He reaches up to adjust the cannula in his nose,

but both of his hands are bandaged and there's no way he can manage it.

"Can I do something for you?"

With one gauze-mittened hand, he gestures toward the tube.

"Can you push it in a little more? Feels like it's sliding down my face and I can't think — can't think straight."

Reaching up, I ease the tube upward as he instructs. "Better?"

"Yeah, thanks, man."

"What do you remember?"

"We were striking the set after they discovered the empty crypt, and I went back to shut down the genny. Simple. Done it a thousand times. When my hand connected with the switch, everything went black." He groans and looks at his hands. "I'll be out of work for months. I just can't—"

"Hey, don't worry about that. I know Mitzy has a fund for things like this. Just don't worry about financial stuff right now. I need you to think back to that moment before walking up to the genny. That's the generator, right?"

He nods subtly. "Yeah, sorry for all the jargon. It's my life."

"Understood. What did you see as you walked toward it?"

He closes his eyes, and I hope he's attempting to recall some imagery and not falling asleep.

Eventually, his eyes ratchet open and he whispers, "There was a wet down. We never wet down by a genny."

"Pardon my inexperience, Mr. Murray. What's a wet down?"

His eyes move toward me, and he seems to see me for the first time. "Right. Wet down is when we hose off pavement or cement to cut the glare. Sounds like it wouldn't work. But trust me. It's a godsend when you're blasting an M90 Max on a huge strip of concrete. Trust me, man."

"I do. And why is it odd that there was a wet down by the genny." I'm getting the hang of this lingo. Mitzy will be thrilled.

"Water conducts electricity, man. That's grip/electric 101."

"Understood. Anything else that seemed strange or out of place? A feeling of cold, a strange sound?"

Mr. Murray looks at me as though I've lost my mind. He might be right. Trying to pin the crime on a ghost I'm not even sure exists sounds like lunacy.

He shakes his head. "That's the only thing I can remember. Something had to be hooked up wrong. Somehow the juice was looping back on the genny. That's the only way it'd be possible."

"Thank you for your time, Mr. Murray. I'll get this information to the rest of the team, and we'll get an electrician out there to look at the genny before it's moved."

He attempts to nod, but fatigue wins the day and he drifts off into a fitful sleep. His bandaged hands twist and turn.

Poor guy.

Glancing at my watch as I walk out of the ward, I note the time. Mitzy should've checked in five minutes ago.

Stuffing the panic down, I stop at the desk, thank Amanda, and practically sprint back to my car as I fire off a text to my partner. "You're five minutes late reporting, Deputy Moon."

To my great relief, the phone rings.

"Simmer down, Harper. I was deeply focused on my ghost hunting. I'm checking in now."

"And?" This woman's dramatic timing is infuriating.

"And, nothing. Nada. Bupkus. No ghost. No magic. No Rory. We might be barking up the wrong tree."

I can't stop the sigh of relief that escapes. "That means we're looking for a killer. Attempted killer at this point. But I'm gonna ask Juárez to assign security to Murray's room at the hospital. I'm sure she can spare another guy or gal."

"Yeah. Everyone's acting strange around here. Should I question the grip that pulled the broom-handle move?"

"I'll take care of it. I've got Murray's statement and I'm on my way."

"Oh! Well, if Harper the Hero is on his way, then I'd be the last person to jump in and attempt to handle anything for him." Her wry chuckle fills the Nova.

"Keep everyone away from the genny. Sounds like it was definitely tampered with. We need to get one of our own electricians to take a look at it before anyone moves it."

"No problem. I'll call Twiggy. She knows everyone."

"See you in five, Moon."

There's a slight pause, and for a minute I worry she hasn't heard me.

"I just hit the timer, Harper. You better get after it."

That woman. Chuckling, I stomp the accelerator and point all 275 horses toward the funerary grounds.

CHAPTER 11
MITZY

BY THE TIME ERICK ARRIVES, I've already got an electrician en route, and I made sure two grips created a field-expedient barrier around the generator with apple boxes, C-stands, and stingers. For the uninitiated, those are wooden crates that folks stand on, 3-legged metal stands used by grips, and extension cords.

"Looks like you've got everything under control, Moon. When will the electrician get here?"

"Oh, he can't make it until next week."

Enjoying the expression on Erick's face, I let the shock and disappointment sit for a couple of seconds.

"At least that's what he said, until I offered to double his rate and add a $500 bonus if he got here in less than half an hour."

Erick's shoulders relax, and he scoffs. "Money talks. Just when I think human decency is the core, you come swooping in and prove me wrong."

"Not necessarily. It was my human decency that offered him the extra money." I flash my eyebrows.

"Touché, Moon. Touché."

"Let's go talk to that grip, all right?" I hook my arm through his elbow and walk him toward the beast of a man who saved Mr. Murray's life.

"This is Rabban. Not his real name. He's named after that character in the Dune movie. You know the reference?"

To my surprise, Erick nods. "Only from the old-school one. Sting's brother or cousin or something. Right?"

"Nicely done, Harper." With that, he takes the lead.

"Any idea who might've touched the genny before Murray got there?" Erick jerks a thumb over his shoulder toward the cordoned off generator.

The brooding beast of a man shakes his head sharply. "Sparky don't let nobody touch the genny but himself. Anybody went near the thing would get straight up fired."

I exchange a glance with Erick and take over. "Anybody in the crew have a problem with Murray? Personally, or professionally?"

This question does not get an immediate answer. Rabban thinks long and hard before offering a curt reply. "No idea, man."

Without warning, the antique mood ring on my left hand forms a frozen circle around my finger. With as much subtlety as I can muster, I glance at the smoky cabochon and have the horrible misfortune of seeing the moment when I took the cursed ring from Rory's deceased hand.

Shaking my shoulders to release the invisible, icy grip on my hand, I clear my throat and announce, "Hey, I need to get back to Silas and Bristol. Can you wrap things up here—"

"Everything okay, Moon?" Erick's gaze flicks to my left hand.

"Yeah. Copacetic. Gotta run."

The muscles in his jaw flex with tension. "Don't forget to report in."

"Huh?" My thoughts are already on my next move, and I've clearly forgotten the rules of my honorary deputy-ship. "Right. Copy that."

Without another thought for Harper, I dash to my Jeep and race back toward Rainbow's End.

Upon my arrival, I'm shocked to discover Silas Willoughby enraptured by a bag of bright orange cheesy puffs, as Bristol's fingers fly across her keyboard.

"Well, sorry to interrupt your slumber party." I stop to place a hand on my hip.

I can't remember ever seeing guilt on my mentor's face, but this snapshot is a precious gemstone that I won't soon forget.

"Mizithra. You've returned sooner than expected." He crumples the bag closed and searches for anything with which to wipe his orange-powder-coated hands.

Sensing some sincere distress, I grab a paper towel from the small kitchen and hand it to Silas. "I need to be getting you back to your place. We can talk on the way."

He gratefully accepts the paper towel and busies himself with dairy-dust removal. Meanwhile, Bristol is bursting with information.

"Dude. You're not gonna believe what we found."

I love that she's including Silas in her explanation. People who take all the credit for themselves and never recognize their support group rub me the wrong way. "Go on."

"That antique chick's name totally *is* Opal Williams. Erick was, like, spot on, you know?"

Holding my tongue, I wait for additional details.

"She sold off most of the stuff in less than a week. Packed up the rest of it and vanished. It took me an hour to track down Rory Bombay's deets. Once we, like, uncovered the Bombay International Antiquities Corporation, the universe was low-key vibing with me."

"All right." I'm pretty sure that means she dug up some good stuff. "Where can we find Opal Williams?"

"I don't think we can, boss. There's no trace. She, like, jumped ship and it's gotta be one of those 'we don't send 'em back' countries, like, when that Snowden dude skipped, bro."

"Come on. Really? Do I need to get on a plane?"

Silas at long last finishes with his chore, gets to his feet, and shuffles toward me. "Despite our predisposition to suspect the worst of Rory Bombay, I believe this is what you would call a 'dead end.' If Opal Williams has vanished into thin, international air, it is highly unlikely she has any connection to the events at the mausoleum."

"I might have agreed with you a couple of hours ago, but there was an attempted murder. The gaffer — the guy who literally knows everything there is to know about electricity — got *electrocuted* on the set. Barely survived. That sounds like Rory to me."

Silas harrumphs. "Join me in the Jeep, Mitzy."

He thanks Bristol for her adroitness — his word, not mine — and exits the trailer.

"Bristol, keep digging. If you find any way to contact that woman, text me. I want to hear from her own honey-coated, southern-belle mouth she didn't have anything to do with this."

My sidekick pops a salute. "Copy that."

After joining Silas in the vehicle, I head to the Gothic mansion across town, outside Pin Cherry city limits.

"What information do you bring?"

"I had a vision. I saw Rory's cursed ring — in my hand."

Silas quietly smooths his mustache while his other hand presses on various locations on his tweed jacket. Perhaps checking for supplies; perhaps he just has an itch.

"What are you thinking, Silas?"

"It's quite risky, although I believe I could sufficiently protect you. On the other hand, I should trust my instincts. Too risky. I am risk averse at this juncture."

"Silas, if we don't get ahead of this, we're being taken for a ride straight to Dante's dumpster fire. You and I both know if Rory Bombay is involved in this attempted murder, it's not the end of the line. We need to uncover what he's thinking. What post-apocalyptic, resurrection scenario he envisioned."

Silas exhales with a quiet moan. "A posthumous plague could indeed create an unimaginable disaster."

The alliteration on posthumous plague tickles my funny bone and, despite the seriousness of the topic, I burst out laughing as I turn onto Willoughby's drive.

"Whatever you need me to do . . . I'm ready. I can handle it, Silas."

"We shall find out together."

Inside the library, Silas presses the great toe on the life-sized marble statue of Greek and Egyptian mythology.

Next, his right hand traces sigils in the air as he chants a series of phrases.

Leaning into my new language-related abilities, I can sort out Polish, Latin, German, perhaps Fijian, and at the very end, oddly, English.

The vault door slides open, and a thick force field envelopes us. If I attempt to move my hand quickly, it's locked to my side. A slow random move passes through the protections.

Silas makes note of my efforts. "It is designed to protect from intentional harmful advance toward the contents. I shall retrieve Mr. Bombay's dangerous ring. Stay where you are."

No problem. It's obvious I haven't developed the abilities necessary to move through this alchemical working unhindered, in the smooth, unrestricted way of Silas.

He returns, secures the vault, and pulls back one of his richly hand-knotted rugs, revealing a gleaming inlaid brass pentagram the size of a dinner table for eight.

"Place yourself in the center. Breathe deeply."

My mentor walks counterclockwise around me. A psychic hit informs me he's casting a circle of protection. "Silas, you told me you don't practice magic."

"The depth and breadth of my knowledge continue to shock you. That is understood. When your grandmother took part in the coven, I discovered it helpful to track the scope of her actions. As we worked together to find the means to tether her spirit to the bookshop, it became necessary for me to master the finer points. What I will ask you to do tonight requires absolute protection without interruption."

"Copy that. What are you going to ask me to do?" My eyes immediately lock onto the small pouch in his hand. A pouch which, I am certain, contains a cursed chunk of rare meteorite encircled by ancient runes — the potent ring once belonging to Rory.

"The circle is cast. I will cut a door with a ceremonial athamé and place this ring on your finger.

After which I will reverse my actions and exit. Once the circle is again complete, I will ask you to channel Rory Bombay. The circle will protect you from possession, as well as the possibility of his spirit latching onto you in any way. However, it will appear as though you are he. You will speak with his voice, and he will reveal his plans. Once we have the information we require, I will reenter the circle and remove the ring. This must be done in a particular order. It is imperative you remain protected at all times."

"Can't I just take the ring off myself?"

"Perhaps. But in my experience, when one channels a spirit from the other side of the veil, the connection to the object serving as the spirit's point of entry is too strong to overcome. I am here to protect and guide you. Are you prepared to take this risk, Mizithra Achelois Moon?"

This feels more solemn than my wedding vows. "If it means no one else will get hurt, I am."

Silas, ever the realist, replies, "It means no such thing. If you are able to unmask his plan, it will at best give us an increased chance of thwarting it. I offer no other guarantees."

"Fine. I've got my money on thwarting. Put the ring on my hand."

Silas removes an ancient silver athamé from his coat. As he pierces the circle of protection around me, bright-blue electricity crackles against the blade. He begins at the floor; slices upward to the left, and down. Creating an energetic door. He enters and reverses his actions. Effectively closing the door behind him.

"We must place this ring on your right hand. It is my recommendation that you remove the ring representing your nuptials. Love is a powerful bond, as you know. That energy could interfere with an accurate message from beyond."

"You'll keep it safe, right?"

"Indeed." Removing the precious rose gold and opal ring, I place it in the breast pocket of my mentor's jacket, as he indicates.

He then slips a protective glove on his left hand and removes the cursed ring from the small bag.

Silas slides it onto the index finger of my right hand, mumbles something I fail to discern, and exits the circle using the athamé and the method previously described.

Once the energetic door is sealed, the circle of protection hums in circumference around me.

The ring sits lifeless on my finger. Nothing happens.

Willoughby's powerful voice commands, "Rory Bombay, also known as Frank Freeman, we call you to this circle immediately. State your business on the mortal plane and your plans for the souls of this world."

The hairs on the back of my neck stand on end. The souls of this world? That seems a little far-reaching—

"How delicious."

An all-too-familiar fear roils my stomach as a dull reddish glow emanates from the vile ring on my right hand.

"My favorite psychic plaything and her hapless wizard have disturbed my eternal slumber. What game shall we play?"

A voice not my own is definitely emanating from my lips. My connection to my Mitzy-ness is dissolving.

Silas pushes onward. "Mr. Bombay, thank you for joining us. What plans have been put in motion by the opening of your crypt?"

The wicked, velvety laugh glides through my body. Rory's voice replies, "Someone actually opened the crypt? Oh, I chose well in Opal Williams. If only I could offer her further reward."

Willoughby lifts both of his hands, and swirling green energy hops from his palms to the circle of protection. "What are your plans?"

I can feel Rory's spirit resisting.

Maybe I can push internally and help to direct the spirit's energy.

A growing rhythm crushes my free will.

"You have no idea the power that exists beyond death, Mitzy. You should've joined me when you had the chance. We could rule the underworld like Hades and Persephone."

My eyes snap to the doorway of the library as Erick Harper enters. The sliver of me that is left inside this husk attempts to scream out a warning.

Too late.

Rory's nefarious green eyes lock onto the intruder. "Sheriff Harper! I was waiting for your arrival. It wouldn't be proper to start the party until the gang's all here."

The spirit moves my body closer to the edge of the circle and hurls unimaginable threats at my confused husband.

"Mitzy? Are you—" Erick's jaw hangs in midsentence.

"This foolish woman has blundered into exactly the place I had hoped to bring her on my own. It's a shame you could never 'seal the deal,' Sheriff. Now Mizithra and I will be joined in eternal bliss."

Stepping within millimeters of the circle's shimmering edge, Erick's eyes burn with fury as he looks above me. He must be gazing eye to eye with whatever ethereal version of Rory exists.

"That's where you're wrong, Bombay. Mitzy

and I *are* married. She's not yours for the taking. She never was."

Erick's words temporarily shift the balance of power. I have control over my body. Removing the ring feels like a valid option.

No. Not yet.

We need the information.

The flash of control vanishes, and the vengeful spirit communicating through me lifts my left hand.

"Never play poker with me, Harper. Clearly, Mitzy wears no wedding band."

Silas puts a hand on Erick's shoulder and attempts to hold him back from the circle of protection. Erick shrugs off his hand and stares daggers at Silas. "Where's her ring?"

"It is safe." Silas points to his breast pocket. "She had to remove it to—"

Erick looks hard into my eyes the minute he sees the strange ring on my index finger. "What is that? What is she wearing?"

Willoughby attempts to explain, while the spirit of Rory Bombay surges with vehemence and spite.

"If your lies are in fact truth, then I shall take your bride to the grave. Mitzy will be mine in the afterlife, as I always intended." Rory compels me backward, to the center of the pentagram, and I fight against his will as my own hands encircle my throat.

His vindictive laughter fills my ears. The thudding rhythm grows louder.

Choking and gasping, I'm unable to call for help.

My vision swirls, and a foggy tableau plays out.

Silas presses Erick back, and attempts to cut an energetic door.

Things do not go as intended.

An explosion of power rocks my world when Erick slams through the ring of protection and darts toward me.

He yanks my hands from my throat, grabs the cursed ring, and rips it from my finger. The ring skitters across the floor.

Erick cradles me tenderly, but his words hold only terrified fury. "Start talking, Moon."

Fade to black.

CHAPTER 12
ERICK

Scooping Mitzy into my arms, I turn my impotent anger on Silas Willoughby. "What have you done? What are the two of you playing at?"

By way of an answer, Silas shoves an enormous stack of books off a large oak table behind him and motions for me to place Mitzy there.

"I need to get her to a hospital, Silas."

"Mr. Harper, there are things you do not understand. When you pierced the circle of protection, you exposed Mitzy to a jolt of power her psychic abilities are too tender to withstand. I need to examine her before any allopathic doctor tends to what may physically ail her. We must also ascertain what happened to the spirit she was channeling."

Every instinct I possess, from many years of training in the Army and law enforcement, tells me to rush her to a hospital. Forcing myself to take a beat, I have to recognize that Silas is right. I have no idea what I'm dealing with in this realm.

Defeated, I lay the limp form of my wife on the table as Silas shoves past me. He pulls a vial from his pocket and pours a strange amber liquid into her mouth. His hands move above her and seem to feel the very air surrounding her motionless body.

"The spirit is fully disconnected. At least you do not have to worry about Rory Bombay's interference on this side of the veil. Fortune smiles on the brave, I suppose." Silas fixes me with a stare that chills the marrow in my bones.

All I can muster is a stuttering excuse. "Look . . . I'm sorry. I was trying to—"

His fiery gaze lessens. "I imagine, had I been young and impulsive, I would've reacted in much the same way. While you may have prevented her untimely death, you've trapped her in a strange energetic purgatory. She is neither here nor there. I have experienced nothing of this nature in all my years dealing with the arcane. Take her to the hospital. They will keep her on fluids and nutrients. I shall research to the ends of the earth to discover how to bring her back."

I swear my heart stops beating. "What?" A heavy thud in my chest shows I'm still alive, but my brain can't process what I'm being told.

"She is alive, Erick. Perhaps due to your actions. Whether I can return her to consciousness in this realm is a matter I must investigate. Please, take her to the medical facility and allow me to begin my research."

"Are you telling me you don't know if you can bring her back?"

"Indeed."

My throat tightens, and I have to fight hard against the demons of PTSD from the battlefield.

Mitzy is still alive. She has a thready pulse, but she's alive. That's what I need to remember.

Scooping her into my arms, I carry her to the Nova parked out front. I hold back my tears by will alone. Now is not the time to think about the soldiers we lost over there. I plan to stay strong and check in with Silas every few hours. I'm counting on this strange little man's abilities to bring Mitzy back to me.

As I drive to the hospital, I review the facts of the case to distract myself from the gaping void. Mitzy said there was no ghost at the mausoleum. Silas said Rory's not on this side of the veil. There's little chance Rory Bombay is involved. The independent electrician reported that the copper grounding wire on the generator wasn't clamped to the grounding rod. He said it was a rookie mistake. That means it wasn't an accident. I'll have to check in with Bristol to see what she uncovered, but I plan to turn my attention to the wholly human cast and crew.

My gut knots. What am I going to do? Tears press relentlessly, and I swallow hard to keep them at bay.

When I step through the doors into the emergency waiting room, Amanda catches my eye across the lobby.

She picks up the phone and her voice crackles over the intercom. "Gurney. Emergency room lobby. Stat." Turning to me she asks, "What happened?"

I'd love to say I have no idea, but that won't help Mitzy. "It seemed like an electrical shock."

Amanda hesitates, but nods. "I'll let the doctor know."

The door bursts open as two orderlies wheel a gurney toward me.

Placing Mitzy on the crisp white linens brings another wave of emotion.

I'm losing this battle. I don't know how much longer I can hold on.

As I attempt to follow the orderlies through the door, Amanda catches my arm. "Erick, let us do our job. Leave your number with me. I'll update you as soon as she's able to have visitors."

Dutifully, I type my number into her phone.

"But . . ." Emotion tightens my throat and my voice vanishes.

"I know. I know. I promise I'll call you the second there's anything to report."

She gently turns me toward the door.

Stumbling into the parking lot, my vision swirls and clouds behind a curtain of tears.

My heart wants to drive back to the cemetery and start cracking skulls until someone confesses. No. That's vengeance talking. I need facts. Cold hard facts that will result in a conviction and life in prison for whoever's guilty.

I need to get squared away.

My entire life, one person could always get me back on the straight and narrow.

Collapsing onto the driver's seat, I grab my cell phone. "Ma, it's Ricky."

DRIVING AWAY FROM THE HOSPITAL IN A DAZE, I can't seem to make a decision. As I turn onto Main Street, all I can think is, "What would Mitzy do?"

Well, what Mitzy did was get herself knocked unconscious, fooling around with otherworldly powers, and some alchemist who I'm starting to worry may not have had her best interests at heart.

This is no time to play the blame game. I need

to take some sort of action. Mom was right. Mitzy is a fighter. She'll pull through.

Even though I couldn't tell my mother the truth about what happened to Mitzy, saying she had an accident and was unconscious in the hospital was enough information to get a good lecture from Gracie Harper.

She told me to *do* something. Not to mope around feeling sorry for myself. Okay, Ma. I'm going to the only place that comes to mind. The Bell, Book & Candle. Maybe if I head into Mitzy's old apartment and try to set up the murder board with Isadora, something will click. Something we missed, because we were all focused on the idea that Rory Bombay could somehow be responsible.

Even after his death, that guy keeps screwing up my life. "If I get—"

Focus up, Harper. This isn't a drill. Your wife is in the hospital. An attempted murder was committed on a set supposedly under your security's protection.

Get over to that bookshop and figure it out. You can hardly consider yourself ready to be sheriff of Birch County if you can't solve one crime on your own.

Parking in the available garage, I head into the bookshop through the alleyway door. The pep talk did its job.

I'm done feeling sorry for myself.

Checking the back room and the first floor, I find the place deserted. Twiggy must've closed up as soon as the crew left.

I unhook the "No Admittance" chain, step up the circular staircase, and latch the chain behind me. When I reach the Rare Books Loft, I'm shocked to discover the entire curved mezzanine of books draped in green cloth.

Every bookcase from the far left all the way around to the end of the curving arm on the right is blanketed in hideous lime green. No idea what that's all about. But I've got a mission to complete. No distractions.

Now, to rustle up some support.

Pushing aside a panel of green cloth, I reach up, tilt the candle sconce down, and wait for the book-case to slide open.

The first image to hit me is Pyewacket, who ap-pears to be online shopping. It can only mean one thing.

"Isadora? Are you responsible for Pyewacket's shopping spree?"

I can't hear ghosts or see them, so I'll have to keep talking until she does something I can see.

"Isadora, I've got a big problem, and I need your help. If you're here, please figure out a way to let me know."

The office chair holding the large tan caracal spins and moves toward me. The sight is alarming at best.

"That's enough. I get it. Can you get your 3 x 5 cards and help me set up the murder board?"

The stack of cards on the coffee table stirs, and a pen scratches rapidly across the rectangular white surface.

First question should be no surprise.

"Where's Mitzy?"

With an exhausted sigh, I lower myself onto the brocade chaise sofa. "I can't quite explain what I saw. I showed up at Willoughby's place and found them in the library. Mitzy was standing in the middle of some kind of energy field. But it wasn't Mitzy. The voice coming out of her mouth was the voice of Rory Bombay."

The pen scrapes across another card with remarkable haste.

"Channeling?"

"Hey, I can read what you wrote, Isadora. But I have no idea what they were doing. I got angry and probably said some stuff I shouldn't to the weird voice and then it threatened Mitzy's life and—"

A 3 x 5 card knifes through the air like a throwing star.

I retrieve it from the floor. The message is in all caps. "WHAT DID YOU DO?"

"I made Rory's voice angry, and he tried to take her life. I blasted through that force field and all hell broke loose."

She grabs the original message from the table and floats it in the air right before my eyes.

"Where's Mitzy?" The card is shaking.

"She's at the hospital. She's unconscious."

Another card zooms up to eye level. "What about Silas?"

"Silas is fine. He took a look at Mitzy and gave her something from one of the pockets in his weird coat. Then he told me to take her to the hospital."

The card quivers in the air.

Emotions surge through my veins.

I punch my fist into the arm of the sofa. "I screwed up. This is all my fault. I'm such a horse's a—"

The ghost must be pushing through me. Goosebumps rise on my arms. A second later, the chill shifts to a warm hum, and I can somehow imagine Isadora hugging me. Attempting to offer the only comfort she can.

"I'm sorry, Isadora. If anything happens to Mitzy, I'll . . ." I can't say the words. I don't even want to think the thoughts. "My ma told me to do something. I'd like to get this murder board handled. We can work together. Okay?"

I wait for the pen to scratch across a fresh card. "Yes."

Pushing down the fear, I get to work. "Silas seems pretty confident that none of this was the fault of Rory Bombay. If he's right, and I guess he usually is, we need to figure out who attacked that gaffer."

A card pops up in front of my face. "The who?"

"Sorry, I was overwhelmed with Mitzy's injury and I forgot to tell you about the accident on set. This Gilbert Murray, his job is the gaffer on set. He's in charge of the electrical department, and he got electrocuted. Mitzy said there's no way it was an accident. Somebody stepped in and kept him alive. An outside electrician confirmed the generator wasn't set up properly. We still don't know who set up the electrocution or why they wanted Murray dead. I get that it's usually you and Mitzy who do this, and I don't exactly know how it works, but if I say the names of people involved, can you make out the cards, right?"

Isadora grabs the card that simply says "Yes," shows it to me, and then floats it toward the rolling corkboard.

"Got it. I'm here and ready to tack up the cards. We'll figure out the connections once we get all the names up."

She hands me the first card. Gilbert Murray.

"Yeah. Let's start with the victim." I tack that in the center of the board and rattle off the rest of the names I remember from the production company.

It's slow going, but between the two of us, we get the cards up.

Sitting down on the floor, I rub my fingers together, hoping Pyewacket will offer me a little comfort.

He saunters over, climbs directly into my lap, and pats the car keys in my pocket with his powerful paw.

"Those are my keys, buddy. You wanna go for a ride?"

"Reow." Can confirm.

That's about the only one of his vocalizations that I absolutely understand.

"I don't have time for a road trip, buddy. Anyway, you can't tell me where you want to go."

He climbs from my lap, careful not to dig his claws into my thigh, and emerges a minute later from the closet with a white piece of fabric in his mouth.

As he walks toward me, a 3 x 5 card floats down from above.

"Nurse."

Pyewacket arrives and gently drops a nurse's hat that must be from a costume in my lap.

"I'm not as good at this as Mitzy, but it kinda

seems like you want me to take you to the hospital. Don't take this the wrong way, buddy, but I'm pretty sure they're not going to allow me to take a wild animal into a hospital."

Pyewacket leaps over me and there's scratching and scuttling as he rummages through fabrics in the massive closet. And, unless I'm completely insane, one noise sounds like a drawer opening.

The lean caracal emerges with something red clenched in his jaw.

This time, no otherworldly help is necessary. He drops his prize in my lap and hangs his head in despair.

"*Service animal?* Where did you even get this vest? There's no way this was obtained legally."

He presses his broad, tan head against my chest and I can't resist.

"Okay, buddy. If you're willing to suffer the indignity of wearing this thing, I'll take you."

Pye stands still, cooperative, but avoiding eye contact. We get the service animal jacket secured and I hook the leash to the D-ring on the back.

"Just to be clear. I'm going to hold this leash in my hand. I will never pull it. You're leading me. Sound good?"

"Reow." Can confirm.

CHAPTER 13
ERICK

On my way to the hospital, with Pyewacket riding shotgun, my inner sheriff begins to worry about the legality of this operation. If anyone questions me on the vest, I'm not going to lie.

On the off chance this service animal vest was obtained legally, the only person who could verify that would be Doc Ledo.

Dialing the veterinary clinic, I give my name and ask to speak to him.

"Hey, Doc. You're here on speaker with Erick Harper and Pyewacket."

The animal-centric veterinarian completely ignores me. "Hey, Pyewacket. Anything wrong? You feeling healthy?"

"Reow." Can confirm.

The doctor chuckles. "Now that I have the important stuff out of the way, Mr. Harper, what can I do for you?"

"I'm on my way to the hospital to see Mitzy. It's a long story and I don't have any answers for you."

"Well, I'm sorry to hear that. Please give her my best. Was there something else?"

"Pyewacket wants to see her. At least that's what I think he wants. I'm not quite as skilled at deciphering his wants and needs as my wife. But he dug a service animal vest out of the closet and allowed me to put a leash on it. If anyone asks questions when I get there, can I vouch for its authenticity?"

Again, he addresses the feline. "Pye, I'm sorry your mistress is in the hospital. You've done the right thing."

"Is that a yes, Doc?"

"Sorry, Mr. Harper. I get sidetracked with my patients. Isadora actually got that vest quite legally, and for a hefty sum. I signed all the paperwork myself. You can feel confident in answering any questions. And if they require further verification, you give them my number."

"Thank you, sir. Mitzy will be grateful for the visit."

"I'm sure she will. Who wouldn't be? And don't cause any trouble, Pyewacket. It's been too long since your last nail trimming."

"Re-ooow."

Doc Ledo laughs heartily. "Oh, I know what that means. You both take care now." The call ends.

Pyewacket flexes the claws on his left paw and almost seems to offer a smug grin.

My phone rings. Call it serendipity, but something tells me even if she's unconscious, Mitzy's behind it.

"Amanda? Do you have news?"

"I do. Unfortunately, it's not much. They checked her over from head to toe. All her vitals are stable. She remains unconscious. She's been moved to the third floor. Room 327. I'll check in on her before I go home."

"Thanks, Amanda. You don't have to do that. I'm sure the nurses on three will take good care of her."

"It's no trouble, Erick." Her voice is soft and caring.

"Okay. Thanks."

I end the call and, as the speakers go silent, Pyewacket twists his head toward me and his black-tufted ears twitch with irritation.

"What? She's a nurse at the hospital. What's that look you're giving me?"

The right side of his mouth seems to tug upward in a classic expression of disdain.

"I swear on Isadora's grave, there's nothing going on between me and Amanda. She's just the nurse at the ER. We went to high school together. She promised to call me if there was any change in Mitzy's condition."

His gaze narrows, but the large golden eyes still hold a flicker of doubt.

I park near the main entrance and circle the vehicle to get Pyewacket. He jumps out of his own free will, and I delicately retrieve the leash. "Once again, you're leading me."

As though he understands English — and at this point, part of me thinks he does — he leads me toward the main entrance.

At the check-in desk, we cause a stir. A couple nurses look terrified and scatter to the winds, but the two remaining women lean over the counter and coo at Pyewacket as though he were a newborn baby.

If he hisses, our service-animal cover will absolutely be blown.

Sergeant Juárez told me that the first thing she learned working with a canine officer was that your emotions travel through the leash. I focus on deep breaths and steadying my heart rate.

To his credit, Pye maintains his composure.

The front desk approves our entry. We head to the third floor. Once we're alone in the elevator, I update the cat as though we're partners on a mission. "You did great down there. We gotta get through the nurse's station on the third floor and possibly a doctor or two making rounds. Whatever you do, keep your cool. Okay, buddy?"

"Reow." Can confirm.

The elevator doors slide open, and Pyewacket pulls me through like a proud jungle cat parading his prize to the rest of his clan.

Two nurses approach immediately. "Can we pet him? Is he dangerous? Oh my gosh, he's so cute."

I wait for a sign from Pye, and when he carefully sits and presents his forehead, I take that for approval. "You can pet him gently. But we need to get in to see our patient."

They both take tentative swipes, clearly not confident, and smile as we continue toward the desk.

"Hi. I'm Erick—"

"Good Lord! Why in the world did you bring that wildcat in here?"

"Oh. He's not a wild animal. This is Pyewacket. He's a service animal for Mitzy Moon. We got clearance at the front desk. I was told she's in room 327."

The third floor nurse is a decade older than the

gals on the first floor. Her eyebrow arches suspiciously.

I throw down one of what I'm told is my heart-melting grins, and wait.

"Head down to the end of the hall and take a left, sir."

She drops into her seat mumbling something about anything in a vest, but I choose to leave that fight unpicked.

When we enter room 327, all the hope I'd been carrying in my heart smashes like an egg falling on pavement.

Mitzy remains motionless.

Now there are tubes and wires all over the place and three different machines beeping and clicking at various intervals.

Without waiting for permission, Pyewacket leaps onto her bed.

He climbs onto her chest, and, with his large paw, pushes the oxygen mask off her face.

I have no idea what will happen if that machine goes off, so I grab a chair, put the mask over my mouth, and breathe, determined to keep the readings steady while Pyewacket does whatever he plans to do.

He presses his whiskered mouth close to Mitzy's pale lips.

Flashes of childhood horror stories of cats

sucking the breath from infants or stealing their souls pop to mind. Before I met my wife, I never would've believed any of those tales. Now, every crooked nursery rhyme holds a different meaning.

As I continue to breathe through the mask, I watch her features. Despite the significant weight of a caracal on her chest, her lungs rhythmically fill and empty.

Pyewacket continues his careful work. Whatever that is.

As though I'm watching a colorist paint an old black-and-white photo, skin tones return to Mitzy's face, and her lips turn the light-pinkish-red that makes my heart skip a beat.

Pyewacket remains motionless, intent on his task.

Unbeknownst to me, the excitement of seeing the color returning to her face has caused my rate of breathing to increase.

The monitor goes off, and I hear footsteps approaching in the hallway.

"Pye, get off of her. We're gonna get busted."

He leaps onto my lap as I struggle to return the mask to my wife's face. The desk nurse who arched her eyebrow at us earlier walks through the door and crosses her arms.

"Did you receive some emergency medical tech training I'm not aware of, Erick?"

"No. I knocked it off when I tried to kiss her cheek."

And I said I wasn't going to lie!

The nurse approaches and checks the readouts on the various machines before lifting the plastic oxygen mask.

"She's improved since your arrival. Maybe this malarkey about your service animal isn't all a crock."

She unlocks the cupboard, extracts some tubing, and replaces the full-face oxygen mask with a cannula. Flashes of the unconscious Gilbert Murray in another hospital room at this facility race through my mind.

Two down and— No! Don't let yourself think that. You're not defeated. You're on the right track. Now circle the wagons, Harper.

The woman stands in front of me. "Did you hear me, sir?"

"Sorry. I lose my focus when I worry."

"No point in worrying. She's getting the best care. Her vitals are strong. You should go home and get some rest. It's against my better judgment, but this cat has some power. I don't mind if you bring him back tomorrow."

"Reow." Can confirm.

The woman tilts her head, and I can see a flash

of understanding and confusion on her face. "See you tomorrow, Mr. Pyewacket."

He lifts a sweet paw in her direction, and I can hardly contain the chuckle in my throat as she reaches out and shakes it. "Well, aren't you a treasure?"

The nurse takes her leave and, as soon as her footsteps echo in the hallway, Pyewacket leaps to the floor, looks up at me, and snickers. I'm not kidding you. The cat actually snickers.

He drags me out of the hospital, and I drive his royal furriness back to the bookshop.

"Hey Isadora, if you're here, Pyewacket was a big hit. Mitzy made improvements even in the short time we were there. The head nurse on three invited him back. I call that a success."

The pile of 3 x 5 cards on the coffee table stirs. The card bearing the word "Yes" floats joyfully through the air.

As I take in the murder board, I note Isadora has applied the green yarn. Mitzy told me that Isadora doesn't like red yarn, because it makes her think of blood. That's why they always use green.

Evaluating the connections, I wonder if I'm missing something. "Everyone's connected to everyone. How can I make heads or tails of this?"

A pen scratches across the card. "Affairs?"

"Affairs? That seems pretty cliché." I turn to the stack to wait for details. Instead, I hear words.

"Clichés are simply truths that have been overused, dear."

My knees buckle, and I lunge for the sofa. "Isadora. I swear I just heard your voice. Did you say, 'Clichés are simply truths that have been overused, dear'?"

The "Yes" card zips toward me and practically smashes into my face.

"Okay. Let's not go crazy. Maybe it was a one-time thing. I was breathing through Mitzy's oxygen mask at the hospital. Do you think something transferred?"

"Why on earth would you take the poor girl's oxygen mask, Erick?"

"Well. I can definitely hear you. No need to yell. Pyewacket swatted it off her face. I didn't want the alarm to go off, so I kept breathing into it."

Laughter like the tinkling of a hundred tiny bells fills the room.

Why can I hear Isadora? What in the world is wrong with my brain?

"There's nothing wrong with your brain, dear."

"Wait! You can hear my thoughts now?"

"I can. You can hear me and I can hear you! Oh, this is grand! Just grand."

My brain box feels heavy, and I'm quickly succumbing to overwhelm. "I'll head back to the set in the morning and see what I can find out about any affairs. I'm gonna go to the walk-up now. Please don't follow me. I'm pretty uncomfortable right now."

"Uncomfortable? Consider yourself lucky. Only two people in the entire universe can hear me."

Without replying, I push the mother-of-pearl button inside the apartment and wait for the hidden bookcase door to slide open.

As I cross the Rare Books Loft, I breathe a sigh of relief.

I don't think I can take that. I'll keep busy tomorrow and avoid the apartment.

"I heard that, young man."

Sh**.

CHAPTER 14
ERICK

AFTER TOSSING AND TURNING all night, I'm relieved to hear my alarm at 4:30 a.m.

"REE-ow!" The sound of imminent retribution.

Pyewacket does not share my joy. "RE-ow." Feed me.

"Oh crap. Now I can understand the cat." Just when I'd hoped things were getting better, they're getting worse.

"Coming right up, buddy."

Hopping out of bed, I fill his bowl with Fruity Puffs, and make coffee and toast for myself. My usual appetite is absent.

Maybe I can leave a message for Silas. He'll call me when he gets up.

The call doesn't go to voicemail. The phone rings once before the lawyer/alchemist's weary voice answers. "Good morning, Mr. Harper. I wish I had news. The research continues."

"Have you been up all night? Silas, you gotta rest. You're no good to us if you wear yourself out."

"I shall take heed of your advice, Mr. Harper. Perhaps a brief nap would restore my spirit. Any news on Mizithra?"

"Pyewacket and I went to see her at the hospital yesterday." Before I can offer any explanation, a gasp echoes from the speaker. "How did you perform that feat? Perhaps you have powers of your own." Despite the tension, he emits a soft chuckle.

"Ree-ow." Soft but condescending. Pye definitely doesn't want me taking any credit.

"Not me. It was all Pyewacket. He has a service animal vest and Doc Ledo— No, that's not important. But, I might have a power."

Silence seeps through the phone line, and time seems to stand still.

"Do tell, Mr. Harper?"

I break down the hospital visit, the subsequent discussion with Isadora, and my new understanding of Pye's vocalizations. Shifting my weight from one foot to the other, I wait in worried silence for a reply.

"Most interesting. I have read two accounts of such a transfer. But this is highly unusual, in that Mizithra still lives."

An arrow of panic pierces my heart. "What are you saying? Are you saying I'm getting this ghost hearing power because she's dying? That's not okay, Silas. You better find another answer."

Hanging up, I grab my coat and head for the car. Pyewacket attempts to tag along. "Not right now. I'm heading to set. I'll come back later and take you to the hospital."

"Ree-OW!" A warning punctuated by a threat.

As soon as I hit the second-floor landing, it dawns on me that I have no idea where I'm going. It's unlikely the crew would be at the cemetery with that reveal shot totally blown.

"Pyewacket? Pye? They're probably setting up next door. Want to join me in the bookshop? I'm sure Twiggy could use our help."

A streak of tan fur dashes past me, but when I reach the door to the retail store, there's no cat to be found.

Mitzy always talks about Pyewacket using secret passages, so I'll let him find his own way.

The overall energy level on the set is low. Crewmembers are gathered around a long table piled with food, which must be craft services. The scent of nearly burnt coffee hangs in the air.

There's no sign of the other folks Mitzy said were in charge. Heading to the back room, I seek out the real boss. "Mornin', Twiggy. Anything I can do?"

"Where's your sidekick, Harper?"

The color drains from my face, and emotion grips my throat with an iron fist.

The normally standoffish manager steps closer and lowers her voice. "What happened?"

Sticking to the facts and carefully skirting the emotions is the only way I can hold it together.

Twiggy shakes her spiky head and whistles long and low. "Did you tell Bristol?"

The palm of my hand slaps my forehead for at least the tenth time in the last twenty-four hours. "I've been so distracted. I can't keep track of anything. I'll pop outside and call her right now."

Twiggy grabs my arm. "You stay in here and make your call. I'll stand guard in the hall. There are trucks and a whole mess of trouble in that alley."

"My car's blocked in? What if I—"

She pats my arm and hands me her keys. "I'm here for the next twelve to sixteen. You need anything, you take Connor out there on First Avenue, and do what you will."

The kind gesture threatens to open the flood-gates. Leaning into all my training, I stuff the emotions down hard and seal the vault. "10-4."

She steps into the hallway as I reach out to Silas.

"Hate to bother you again, Willoughby."

"Mr. Harper, I shall call you the moment I have answers."

"Don't mind me . . . I'm a wreck. I need Bristol's number. She doesn't know what happened."

"The services she provides may offer you a much-needed distraction today."

It never occurred to me to work with Bristol, but now that Silas mentioned it . . . Why not? "Yeah. I'm sure you're right. Thanks."

He rattles off the phone number, and, for the first time in all my years of knowing the man, I realize he's never sent me a text. Perhaps the last holdout in the known universe. The thought brings a chuckle as I grab a pen and scratch out the numbers on a notepad on Twiggy's desk.

I thank Silas and place the call.

This back room, with its ancient coffee maker, mismatched chairs, and cabinet full of Fruity Puffs brings back a wave of Mitzy-based memories.

Slapping my face and shaking my shoulders, I force myself back to the present. "Hey, Bristol, it's Erick."

"Bro, what's wrong?"

Maybe this psychic bug is spreading. "Mitzy is in the hospital. She—"

"Dude! What? I got deets on Williams. What now?"

"Slow down, Bristol. You and I will work together today. Who's Williams?"

"That chick you mentioned. The Rory woman."

The mention of Rory Bombay's name stiffens my spine, transforming my sadness into instant anger. "Good. Is she local?"

"How'd you know? She's holed up in some sweet property Bombay's company leases on the rez, bro. We can't touch her."

"That's where you're wrong, Bristol. The Hawk Island reservation isn't out of reach. I made a point of making real good friends with the tribal police. I'll pick you up, and we'll head out there together. Can you text me your address?"

"I'm in Rainbow's End, bro. Two trailers down from your bestie, Westie."

My rage is slowly replaced by suspicion and deep concern. If the psychic thing is spreading, maybe that was Rory's plan all along. Everybody knows everything. Chaos. "How do you know about Westie?"

"Totes. Sorry, bro. Mitzy and I hung with him at the Wards, you know? He's gonna run the whole roller rink project with me. You're down, right?"

More confused than ever, I gotta get in the car and drive. "You can tell me about it on the way to the Hawk Island reservation. I'll be at your place in ten to fifteen. You ready?"

"Always, bro. Always."

Stopping in the hallway, I shake the keys at Twiggy. "Thanks again."

"Stay safe, Harper."

Out on First Avenue, I search for her vehicle. When she mentioned Connor, I had no idea what she was talking about. As I walk down the line of vehicles, a series of bumper stickers catch my eye. There are warnings of the robot revolution and the dangers of AI. I figure I've found my quarry.

No key fob for this rig. Not for this girl. Old school key-in-lock only.

The black 1983 GMC Jimmy has a faded camper shell, and the interior sports a serious layer of dog hair. Twiggy has two pups, Bartles and Jaymes, and she agreed to look after Penny Moore's orange tabby cat after the woman's homicide.

A crime my long-lost father committed. Possibly against his will. Maybe one day . . .

Pushing thoughts of my father into a separate vault in my psyche, I head to Bristol's.

Once I pick her up, my phone blows up. Panic grips my heart, and I grab my cell and stare at the screen. "Hey, what's all this stuff you're sending me?"

"All the deets on Williams, bro. In case you need to, like, cram or whatever, before you interrogate her."

"Don't use the word 'interrogation' on the reservation. We're guests. And we would like to visit Ms. Williams. Preferably with a tribal escort."

"Noice. You got it all sorted, dude."

Her positive energy is hard to resist. "Yeah, not my first rodeo."

"No doubt. No doubt. You straight up bagged a rattlesnake at your first one, bro." She offers a "woot woot," and despite the morning's emotional roller coaster, she breaks down my defenses, and I laugh.

Laughter makes me think of Mitzy. The roller coaster takes a plunge.

Bristol taps her fingers on her knee as she gazes out the window. "Seriously, bro. Don't worry about Mitzy, you know? She's hard-core. Like, I know you're captain of the struggle bus right now, but she's got this. Whatever she's doing in this energetic in-between place, she's gonna figure it out. Don't sweat it, bro. Don't sweat it."

Maybe she's right. I've heard plenty of cases where people in comas later report being conscious of everything happening around them.

Experience has taught me one thing about my wife.

Never. Underestimate. Mitzy. Moon.

CHAPTER 15

MITZY - SOMEWHERE IN-BETWEEN

THE LAST THING I REMEMBER is a blast of energy and Erick saving my life — for the millionth time. Don't get me wrong, I've saved his life too. That's what makes us such a great team. But now, I don't know where I am.

No matter how many signals I send to my eyelids, they refuse to open. The only thing I can see are some psychedelic patterns in my imagination.

Colors, movements, snippets of strange songs, and an occasional disembodied voice. I've never taken an acid trip, but something tells me it would be a lot like this.

Every so often, I have the sensation of being touched. Yesterday, or maybe it was two minutes ago — time has no meaning here — I felt a weird pressure on my chest. But instead of pushing me deeper, it felt like it was slowly pulling me toward the surface.

Wild.

Nothing makes sense in this stupid in-between place.

I'm not worried for myself. Erick must be losing it. He's not exactly cool with all this otherworldly stuff. He said as much a few days ago. Or was that last week?

Silas! He must be researching through his library and mine 24/7.

Thing is, I'm no damsel in distress. I'm here. Wherever *here* is. I'm gonna find out everything I can, and then get the heck out of here.

Rory Bombay doesn't have anything to do with that attempted murder. He talks a big game, but I could feel the truth behind his words. He was shocked that he was called from beyond the veil. He may talk a big game — did I already say that?

Where am I?

Right. In-between.

What was I saying?

Opal Williams is no sorceress. In fact, suffice it to say . . .

Suffice it to say. Suffice it. Saaah-ff-ice it. That's fun to say.

Jeezy creezy! It's impossible to focus in here.

I bet Opal doesn't even know how to cast a cir-

cle. If she had anything to do with the missing remains, it was for some utterly mundane purpose.

That thought releases a hit of dopamine.

Fresh colors burst before my eyes, and I seem to
rush down an endless stained-glass hallway.

There's a familiar feel to the pattern in the
glass.

When I try to focus on the pattern, the vision
shifts.

I'm riding on a griffin, and there's an army of
Pegasus — Pegasi — Pegasuses?

It's gone.

This is like *Mr. Toad's Wild Ride*. I can't hold
on to anything.

A distant beeping pierces the in-between.

What's that? A security alarm?

The code. I can't think of the code! Why can't I
remember the code?

Warmth trickles up my left arm, and all the
colors swirl into blackness.

CHAPTER 16

ERICK

As soon as I enter reservation territory, I drive straight to the tribal police headquarters. Not sure if Sergeant Grayskull still works with Hawk Island, but I'm about to find out.

"Bristol, can you wait in the car? I need to see if my contact, Grayskull, still works here and then talk my way onto the land. It's probably best—"

"Dude! You're lightin' me up, right? Grayskull? Like, by the power of Grayskull?" She can't stop snickering.

"Yeah. That's why I want you in the vehicle. I've worked with him a long time, and he's pretty sensitive about some Saturday morning cartoon stealing his family heritage. That's how he puts it."

Bristol bobs her head, and her pom-poms threaten to come loose from her jester's beanie. "No doubt. No doubt. That's cool with me, you know? The writers on that show, like, didn't do their research! Tread lightly. You know what I mean, bro."

I'm probably only picking up half of what she means, but I get the gist. "Yeah. I know what you mean. Sit tight, okay?"

She grabs the seat beneath her and pulls herself down as hard as she can. "Tight. Tight. Tight. You got it, dude."

Chuckling, I exit the vehicle.

When I walk through the front door, three officers turn. None of them is the man I'm looking for. "Excuse the interruption. Do any of you know where I can find Sergeant Grayskull?"

Two of the faces return to their papers in a silent refusal to respond. The third, a young female officer, stands and crosses her arms. "You have no jurisdiction here, Sheriff."

Stepping closer, I glance at her badge. "Sayers? I'm not the sheriff. I'm running for office in the upcoming election, but I'm here as a civilian. Sergeant Grayskull and I worked together, back in the day."

The jovial moon face of my only ally on their force steps from his private office. "Back in the day, eh? Was that a Wednesday, Harper?"

The energy in the room shifts, and my shoulders relax. "Private room? You on detention in there?"

He laughs. "I'm the big chief. The head honcho around here. All them cases I solved for you finally got me a promotion, eh?"

Grayskull's sense of humor is one reason he and I hit it off.

"Oh. I thought you had an excellent memory. Seems like you misplaced a few facts."

He crosses the distance between us in two strides, and we share a firm handshake.

"What can I do for you today, Not Sheriff?"

"Hey, I have a reasonable chance in the upcoming election. We'll be working together soon. Today, I need to have a casual chat with Opal Williams. Would you guide me to her residence?"

The tension returns faster than a lit cigarette can start a forest fire.

Grayskull shifts his weight and sniffs sharply. "You got an appointment with Her Majesty?"

I motion to the room behind him. "Can we talk in your office?"

Grayskull's jovial manner comes to a sudden halt, and he ushers me into his office, closing the door behind us.

"What's going on, Harper?"

"My wife is in the hospital. The only person who possibly has information that could help her is Opal Williams. Can you get me in the door?"

"We'll take my cruiser. I can usually sweet-talk

Opal. What about you? You still got that way with the ladies, eh?"

"We're about to find out." After asking Bristol to continue sitting tight, I hop in Grayskull's vehicle.

As we come over a small rise, I find myself audibly astounded. "When you said Her Majesty . . ."

Grayskull laughs and shakes his head. "I do not mean to be disrespectful, Harper, but some white people . . ."

Before us, a genuine stone castle shimmers on the ridgeline. Parapet walls topped by granite crenellations, two turrets, and an actual drawbridge across a mote. I have to blink my eyes several times to convince myself it's not a mirage. Sadly, it's not.

"How on earth did the elders agree to this?"

Grayskull rubs his thumb along the steering wheel and hums a melancholy tune. "This was a few years back, you know?"

"Okay. But any land lease has to be approved by the Tribal Council, right?"

"Sure. Sure. Approve is a big word, my friend. Every word has a price."

"Williams couldn't possibly have had that kind of money. She was the manager of an antique store. How could she afford to build something like this?"

"Oh no. You misunderstand. Miss Williams did not build this travesty. She *inherited* it."

Confusion furrows my brow. "Rory Bombay!"

He nods and taps his hand twice on the steering wheel. "That's the name. It had escaped me. Also, this was when Leticia Whitecloud was throwing around a lot of weight and money, eh?"

The mention of the nefarious Native American mafiosa unleashes a series of sweet and heart-breaking memories with Mitzy at the casino. So many pivotal moments in my life involved Mitzy. No! I will not start talking about her in the past tense. Silas will figure this out. Mitzy will figure this out. Someone will figure this out.

"Brother, what troubles you?"

Without revealing any details of what exactly landed my wife in the hospital, I give Grayskull a story similar to the one I gave my mother.

"That is rough, my friend. How can Miss Opal help you?"

Uh oh. I should've seen this coming. Mitzy would know exactly what to do. Maybe I can channel her. "It's in the realm of what your medicine man does. Miss Williams could have an object of power . . . Something that could help me wake Mitzy up."

Grayskull takes this information in stride. "Anything to halt the westward journey, eh?"

"I'm not familiar with that reference."

He looks into the distance as he drives. "We believe that when a body dies, the soul journeys westward for four days to reach the spirit world. Someone in a coma is trapped on that road. You need to find something that will turn your wife around and convince her to jump through the flames. To return to you."

"Yeah, that sounds about right. If Opal has something that could do that, I gotta push hard enough to get at it, you know?"

"If she possesses such a thing, we will get it. From what I know about this *inheritance*, it was a loose interpretation, at best. I might be able to use that angle to help you, you know?"

"Thanks. I owe you one."

"Oh, you are looking at the wrong scoreboard, friend. By my count, you owe me three."

It feels good to laugh. "Oh, maybe your old memory isn't as far gone as I thought. Fine. I owe you three."

We stop next to a large security screen and keypad. Grayskull presses a button, and a voice crackles from the speaker. "State your business."

It's a male voice, definitely not Opal Williams.

"Police Chief Grayskull here to see the lady of the house."

"I don't have anything in the books. Who's the other individual in your vehicle?"

"Oh, him? That is my friend, Erick. Local guy, but interested in artifacts, you know?"

There's a long pause, and I have to hold my breath.

The honeyed tones of Opal Williams are the next to grace us. "Well, Chief Grayskull, you come on inside for a nice glass of sweet tea."

The drawbridge ratchets down and thunks firmly in front of us.

My buddy shakes his head and laughs as we drive across.

Part of me waits for a portcullis to drop behind us, but nothing that dramatic happens. Mitzy would've been disappointed.

Security personnel meet us at the vehicle and insist Grayskull leave his sidearm in the car. To my surprise, he agrees without protest. Since they assume I'm a civilian, they don't frisk me. Seems there's a bit of luck on my side.

Opal, resplendent in an emerald-green dressing gown that accents her auburn curls, leads us into a room to the left of the grand entrance. There's a roaring fire and a silver tea-tray service with a three-tier selection of petit fours.

This is unbelievable.

As Opal pours the tea, she makes small talk. "Erick, what type of artifact would make a handsome man like you happier than a pig in mud?"

Deception has never been my strong suit, but my wife's life is on the line, so I take a stab at it. "I did some research on that antique store you used to run in Grand Falls. Were you partners with Rory Bombay?"

Her face is turned away, but the way her shoulders tense tells me everything I need to know.

She hands me a glass of sweet tea and a small plate bearing a selection of delicacies, and offers the same to Grayskull. He politely declines.

"Why, yes. Mr. Bombay and I worked together for some time. We used to love collecting little treasures. I fell apart like a biscuit in gravy when he passed."

Swallowing the bile in my mouth, I summon a few drops of compassion. "Yes. Sorry for your loss. I was disappointed to discover the shop had closed. Do you continue to sell privately?"

There's a gentle tension in her jaw, and her eyes dart once to the side before she replies. "I dabble. What do you fancy?"

Grayskull laces his fingers together and leans back.

I have a small window here. Probably best not to pounce.

"Well, not sure if this is something you'd carry, but I've recently become fascinated with the occult."

That muscle in her jaw flexes harder.

"You don't say. Anything in particular?" The

honey seems to have melted, and her southern drawl is quickly turning sour.

"I'm looking for a necklace that can wake someone from a coma. Have you ever come across anything like that?" I'm completely spitballing. I sure hope this doesn't blow up in my face.

Her jaw softens, and she sips her tea. "Oh, my dear Erick. Are you pulling my leg? You're sneakier than a possum at a picnic."

I chuckle and grin, in what I hope is a disarming way. "Truth is, I have information. If you can help me with my artifact search . . ." I let the promise dangle like a lure on a fishing line.

Opal's demeanor changes. She angles forward like a black widow spider about to trap its prey. "What kind of information?" She corrects herself immediately. Angling away and casually sipping her tea, she continues, "Erick, darling, I don't know what you've heard, but I deal in historical artifacts of great significance, not fantasy and imagination."

Everything in my law enforcement brain strains for a way to keep the lines of communication open with this woman.

"Understood, Miss Williams. If anything changes, please give me a call." As I reach for a card, I realize handing her the Harper and Moon Investigations business card will not help my case. "Darn. I left my last card at the tribal police office."

I give her my number verbally, and she shockingly types it into her phone.

"Now, Mr. Erick. You said you had a piece of information for me."

This doesn't seem like the time to point out she didn't keep her end of the bargain. "Let's consider my information a down payment on future items you might locate for me. You know, since you didn't have the item I was looking for today."

She nods demurely and bats her eyelashes. "Of course, darling."

"Yesterday, a production company opened the crypt of Rory Bombay, a.k.a. Frank Freeman."

Her lip twitches, but she manages a horrified gasp.

"I'm sorry to have to tell you. It was empty."

She presses her hand to her chest. "That sounds like a tall tale. I was there when they laid him to rest. This is ludicrous — I won't stand for — How dare you!" Her indignation echoes from the high stone ceiling.

Getting to her feet, her cloying perfume sweeps over me as she utters her icy demand. "Deputy Grayskull, please escort this man from my property. We have no further business."

Grayskull remains seated and stoic. "Miss Williams, I am the chief of police of the Hawk Island nation. This land belongs to Mother Earth.

You would do well to remember that." He gets to his feet and saunters toward the front door, calling over his shoulder. "Perhaps you can have a look through all that inventory my people carried into your home. Give my friend a call if you find what he needs, eh?"

Dipping my head in what I hope is a gentlemanly gesture, I follow.

As I hold the door for my longtime friend, Opal's frantic movement catches my eye. She's tapping furiously at her cell phone.

The last thing I see before joining Grayskull outside is a look of horror on her petite face.

CHAPTER 17
MITZY – SOMEWHERE IN-BETWEEN

I'M NOT DEAD. I mean, I'm pretty sure I'm not dead. It took me some time, whatever that is, to come to this conclusion.

Blerg. I can't open my eyes. And that's what convinced me this is not death. If I had crossed over, I'd be free. I could look around and float off to any place I liked in the afterlife. Right?

Or, maybe I'd be trapped in Mr. Willoughby's Gothic mansion.

I wouldn't be mad at that. It'd be an awesome place to haunt.

If I'm not dead, then I must be unconscious. And if I'm unconscious, that means hospital.

Oh no! Another wave of wild imagery. It's almost like being trapped in the original "Yellow Submarine" animation by the Beatles. It's crazy!

One minute I'm alive, channeling the spirit of Rory Bombay — Yes, I finally remembered that! Or did I already know that? The next minute, I'm here. Well, wherever *here* is.

If I—

Shoot! I'm floating down a hallway. That stained-glass pattern . . .

The mausoleum! That window on the back wall of the mausoleum.

Wait. Are those people? This is the first time there have been people in my swirly psychedelic trips.

Crapballs! Everything's going dark. Utterly black.

Wait . . . There's a sliver of light.

It's not stable, it's moving around. That's weird. All I know is, don't go to the light.

It's only a flashlight!

Hey, I'm starting to get the hang of this. Something's scraping to the side, and the sliver of light is widening.

Yikes! Someone's opening the crypt!

Wait . . . Am I *in* the crypt?

It's not the film crew. It's nighttime. Yes! It's nighttime, and they're using flashlights!

No way! I'm seeing this as if I were Rory Bombay!

Gross.

Hold the phone!

These are the people who stole the remains!

As the body nears the surface of the crypt, the flashlight illuminates a face standing back while two strongmen do her bidding.

The southern belle chick!

Why on earth would she steal my— I mean, Rory's remains? This is too bizarre.

I've got to wake up! Erick— Grams— Pyewacket! Somebody get me off this crazy thing!

CHAPTER 18
ERICK

GRAYSKULL TAKES THE LONG WAY back to head-quarters. "I am sorry we could not find the necklace you seek, friend. It is good to spend a little time with you."

"I made up that necklace part. Didn't have any idea what I needed. I was hoping she might offer something. She seemed pretty tight-lipped."

"She *inherited* a great deal of money from this Bombay character. Perhaps she wishes to preserve her options." He glances in the rearview mirror and sucks air between his teeth.

"Kudos to her, I guess. It's not like he had any living relatives."

He scowls. "She forgets her place. Opal Williams is a guest of the Hawk Island nation."

"I hear what you're saying. And I haven't forgotten I'm also a guest. Thank you for taking me out there." He nods, and I continue. "She seemed genuinely surprised to hear about the empty crypt. I kinda thought she might've been involved."

Grayskull chuckles. "That woman? Not on your life, eh? She did not lift a finger to move herself into that place. And she has three security people on shift twenty-four hours a day, a personal chef, a maid, and a driver on-call. This is not a woman who gets her hands dirty."

"Good to know. Good to know." I sniff sharply and shake my head.

He points out the new community center and the additional building on the school grounds. "Leticia Whitecloud was not all bad. She did her best for our people. We learn to take the good with the bad, you know?"

"You do. I know. Keep in mind that Mitzy runs a philanthropic foundation. If there's anything that we can do for you, or the kids, let me know, okay?"

"10-4."

He pulls into his spot in front of the station, and we exit the vehicle. Grayskull comes around to my side and hugs me firmly. "I will ask the elders to pray for Mitzy. We are not unfamiliar with her. She is a good soul."

I return the embrace and choke back emotion. "She'd appreciate that. We both would."

Bristol can barely contain herself when I get back in the car.

"What happened? Did you smoke her out? Did she flip on her old boss? I gotta have the deets, bro."

"Miss Williams is either the consummate actress or less informed than we assumed. She didn't take the bait on my offer to buy occult items from her, and she seemed genuinely shocked to hear Rory Bombay's remains are missing."

"That's tragic, dude. Totes tradge. What's our next move, boss?"

"Head back to the walk-up. I promised Pyewacket another trip to the hospital today. He's not the kinda guy you want to disappoint."

She laughs openly. "No doubt. No doubt."

"You're welcome to pop over to the set. They know you're working for Mitzy now. You can drop in anytime."

"Noice. I'll hold that card until I need it, you know?"

"Okay. Do you want to join us at the hospital?"

Her body language is hard to read. It always seems upbeat, but sort of in a forced way.

"That'd be sweet. I mean, not that it's good that she's in the hospital. No. I mean, oh sorry, bro. You know what I mean."

"I know what you mean." Bristol's entertaining. I'll give her that.

The cul-de-sac beside the bookstore is loaded with white trailers, and First Avenue has bobtail trucks parked back to back. Bristol leans forward and shakes her head. "Looks like we're gonna have to park at the agency, bro."

"Yep. Looks like it. I sure hope Pye is feeling cooperative."

Continuing down First Avenue, I make the left into Harper and Moon Investigations, only to find the parking lot nearly filled with crew vehicles. Pulling right up to the front steps, I hop out and a PA accosts me. "Sir, you can't park here. This is for Tansy Truth crew parking only."

"Good morning. What's your name?"

"Um, Chad. Why?"

"Chad, I'm Erick Harper." I point to the shingle above the office door.

His face registers no recognition. He seems frozen in a command loop. "Chad, I own this property and the parking lot. Which means I can park wherever I want. You're welcome to wedge as many cars in here as you'd like. Just make sure Bristol and I always have a clear path in and out. Understood?"

He rubs the button on his radio, unsure if he should take instructions from someone outside the crew hierarchy. Eventually, he caves. "Copy that."

"Thanks, Chad. We won't be here long. We're gonna pick up my cat and head out." Again, he seems baffled by this information and fails to respond.

We leave him to sort out the details and head inside the office for a quick cup of coffee while I check emails.

There are none. "Well, that was easy. Let's get over to that set."

Bristol's pom-poms bounce excitedly as we walk the few short blocks to the bookstore.

After we navigate around the grip/electric trucks in the alleyway, we enter through the side door and do our best to stay out of the way as crewmembers lug equipment in and out. The director catches sight of us, pops out of his chair, and marches over. He points to Bristol. "You, I saw with Mitzy. You, I'm not sure about. I'm the director, Noah Madson. State your business." He opens a pack of nicotine gum and throws two pieces in his mouth.

"Mitzy's husband. I was at the cemetery."

His eyes widen with recognition, and his expression is immediately replaced with frustration. "We just keep hitting one dead end after another. First, this paranoid Twiggy woman won't let us film in the Rare Books Loft without green screen on everything, and then we open an empty crypt! The writers are threatening to strike, the script is in revision again, and I'm stuck shooting scenes I'm not even sure I'll be able to use. Just stay out of our way."

Careful to use the proper jargon, I reply, "Copy that."

Noah returns to his chair, studies the monitors, and shouts at the camera crew.

"Our best bet is to get Pyewacket and get outta here. What do you think, Bristol?"

She turns to answer. Instead, her jaw drops as the alleyway door flies open and a screaming Shawna Fenty runs in. Shawna trips over a cable and launches headlong.

Instinctively, I lunge forward to catch her. The white-blonde hair brings a flash of warmth to my face. Of course, when Shawna's pointy, skeletal face stares up at me, the spell is broken.

"Wow, you must be the real deal. You're the guy the Timothy Barber character is based on, right? Thanks for saving me, big guy." She drags her hand over my chest, and my skin wants to crawl away.

"It's instinct, Miss Fenty. What were you shouting about?"

The seductive grin vanishes, and her eyes dart in horror. "Gabby's dead!"

I have no idea who Gabby is, but Bristol takes the lead. "Come on, Harper. I got this."

Bristol busts out of the bookshop, takes a hard left, and I'm on her heels.

She sprints around the corner to the cul-de-sac at the end of Main Street, jogs up the steps of the trailer in the center, and stops abruptly when she steps inside. She turns and covers her mouth. Her face is a little green around the gills.

"Step outside. I'll take care of this."

Approaching the body, I take three quick photos on my cell phone. A nearby rack of clothing stands almost bare. Costumes lie haphazardly on the floor. It's likely Gabby fought her attacker.

As I lean in, Mitzy's invaluable training comes in handy. I note the red-soled Christian Louboutins, which have been buckled together and used to strangle this woman.

Her perfect silver-polished manicure is marred. The left hand, lying limp on her chest, displays a dark red substance under the fingernails. "Bristol, secure the area. I'm calling Sheriff Paulsen."

CHAPTER 19
MITZY – SOMEWHERE IN-BETWEEN

MY SWIRLING PSYCHEDELIC VISIONS have taken form. Hooray?

Nope.

When I glance around, I wish they hadn't.

The only thing keeping hope alive is the flimsy belief that I'm unconscious in a hospital bed. What day is it?

In the corner of my mind sounds the echo of Rory Bombay promising to rule the underworld with me at his side. Based on this current "trip," his dream, my nightmare, has come true.

I sit upon a golden throne, and a familiar charm bracelet hangs on my left wrist.

"Where did this come from?" I shake my wrist in frustration.

"A gift, my Queen. What do you think of this

castle I built for you? A fitting wedding present, no?" He strokes his chin, and his devilish emerald eyes sparkle with satisfaction.

The slimy, controlling voice raises the hairs on the back of my neck. "Wedding present? Have you lost your mind? I would never marry you."

He flashes his right hand in my direction, and the cursed ring that once resided in the vault of Silas Willoughby again rests on the hand of this maniac.

"Do you like it? I knew if I made a bit of magical mayhem, you and your foolish wizard would open the vault. Now that I've rewritten history, things are going to be different. We'll use your powers to locate the Oracle of Return. Once I reclaim my rightful spot on the other side of the veil — Oh, the possibilities are limitless, my love." He leans toward me with a salacious grin.

Ew! My skin wants to crawl off my body! "I am not, and will never be, *your* love." How can I get a message to Silas?

"Darling, your mother came to you in a vision and spoke of the Oracle of Return. Remember? I'm sure your sweet mum must've given you a location. You simply must share it with your eternal life partner." He gives me pleading puppy-dog eyes.

"You can keep me prisoner for all of eternity, *Frank*. I'll never help you. Never." Using his true birth name sends a flash of anger darting through his viridian eyes.

"Trust me, my love. Eternity is exactly how long we have." His tone is clipped. Final.

This can't be happening!

The castle walls swirl into rivers of color. I'm floating.

No!

A stained glass window appears.

Am I dead? Have I been here before?

Maybe this is my Hell loop.

The empty crypt opens, and Rory's controlling voice beckons me back.

No way I end up in the *Bad Place*. I changed when I came to Pin Cherry Harbor. I've used my powers for good. Why would I be in Hell?

I need to get a message to — ANYONE!

A familiar warm feeling flows up my arm, through my body, and the images swirl to darkness.

CHAPTER 20
ERICK

"Paulsen, we've got a body on set. Main Street cul-de-sac, south of the bookshop."

Paulsen offers her usual squawk of resistance, but I hold my ground. "Look, this woman was strangled by some of her own wardrobe. After the attempted murder at the cemetery yesterday, I'd think you'd be a little more interested. Someone is targeting this production."

She offers one additional protest and hangs up.

Seconds later, I hear the sirens from up the block.

Paulsen shouts as she approaches the trailer. "You. The one in the beanie. Out of my way."

The current sheriff storms into the trailer with her right hand on her gun. And stops cold. Her expression tells me she clearly didn't believe me.

Stepping back from the body, I motion for her to take over. "Signs of a struggle." I gesture to the empty rack and the clothing on the floor. "Looks like she got a good swipe at her attacker. Be sure to have the medical examiner swab for DNA."

"Don't tell me how to do my job, Harper. And it is still *my* job. You're a civilian, tampering with evidence at my crime scene. Clear out."

"No need to ask me twice. All yours, Paulsen."

As I pass Deputy Johnson, I tilt my head toward him and whisper, "You're gonna need backup. There are over forty people in the cast and crew. You'll need to hold them all and get their statements. Make it seem like your idea."

Johnson grins broadly and nods his head.

As we round the corner from the cul-de-sac at the end of Main Street onto First Avenue, Bristol dares to speak.

"Who are we questioning first?"

"I don't remember everything Shawna was shouting, but seems like she was yelling for Gordon Fall. Isn't he the executive producer? We should start with him." When I reach for the front door of the bookshop, Bristol puts a hand on my arm. "Hey. What do you know about this door, bro?"

We stand and admire the thick wooden door, intricately carved with a variety of scenes. There's one of a centaur chasing a maiden through a delicate woodland; another of a faun playing a flute for a family of rabbits dancing around his cloven hooves; there's the shadow of a winged horse passing in front of the moon; and finally, a wildcat stalking a small boy — a cat who bears a striking resemblance to Pyewacket.

"Not much. Mitzy said Silas was vague about the origins. He claimed it was a gift to Isadora. But he's never explained how Pyewacket got on there."

Bristol crouches and inspects the intricate carving of Robin Pyewacket Goodfellow, which includes the mysterious scars over his left eye. "That's totally Pye. With all the tea Mitzy's been spilling, makes me wonder if he's, like, even a cat, you know?"

That thought had occurred to me, but I've never shared it with anyone. I didn't want to sound crazy. "Between you and me, I've wondered the same thing."

She gets to her feet, pulls off her beanie, and bows her head.

I have to ask, "Bristol, what are you doing?"

"Oh, you know. Just a moment of silence for Gabby. We ran into her the other day at craft service. She was totally cool. Mitzy told Gabby she was the author."

"What? What did Gabby say? Do you remember the details?"

Bristol's usual rhythmic voice vanishes and, as though she's reading from a script, she repeats the conversation.

GABBY
"Huh. What do you think of the casting?"

MITZY
"I was a little surprised, but I have no idea what appeals to the TV audiences."

GABBY (laughing)
"That waif had an affair with the showrunner. Got some pillow-talk dirt on him and blackmailed her way into a lead role. Trust me, she was not the director's first choice."

                    MITZY
            "Wow. Are you sure?"

                    GABBY
        "Yup. Hate to be a cliché, but
        Gordon spilled his guts once I
         started, um, seeing him."

                    MITZY
        "Oh. And here I was thinking,
          everything they say about
          Hollywood sets was an
              exaggeration."

GABBY   indicates   MITZY'S   tennis
shoes.

                    GABBY
        "Now those are the shoes of a
           private investigator."

GABBY   shows   her   Christian
Louboutins.

            GABBY
"These are the shoes of a kept
            woman."

            MITZY
"You look like you can
take care of yourself — if you
            need to."

            GABBY
"Yup. I know where all the
bodies are buried." (Takes a
beat) "Metaphorically
speaking."

"She said that? She said she knew where all the bodies were buried?" Then I nod in appreciation. "Excellent memory, by the way."

Bristol tugs her beanie on and bobs the pompoms. "No doubt. No doubt. But, like, Gabby was just goofing, you know?"

"What if she wasn't? It could be a motive."

"Dude. You just gave me the chills, bro." Bristol rubs her hands up and down her own arms. Her fingerless gloves scratch against the fabric of her hoodie.

Giving the hand-carved door a pull, I discover it's secured. "That explains why Shawna ran all the way around to the alley. Let's get inside and look for Gordon Fall."

Bristol falls in behind me, and we head back to set. We ask every crewmember we pass the same question. "Have you seen Gordon Fall?"

After following a wild goose chase of dead-end tips across the entire set, I throw my hands up in frustration. "He's not here. That's not normal, is it?"

Bristol shakes her head vehemently. "No way, bro. That dude is like super baller around here, you know?"

"Maybe he overslept." My voice holds little conviction.

The robotic voice returns. "Early is on time. On time is late. Late is fired."

"What's that?"

"That's from the PA's handbook. If he's not here, something's wrong."

Dragging my thumb along my jaw, I scratch at my stubble and search for a sliver of a clue. "What if—?"

"What if he's the killer, bro?" Bristol nearly pops out of her skin.

"My thoughts exactly." Opening the metal door to the alley, I turn. "Bristol, with me."

We jog back to Harper and Moon, nod to the PA on parking lot detail, and hop in Twiggy's vehicle. I'll apologize to Pyewacket later about the missed trip to the hospital.

"What hotel are the cast and crew staying at?"

"Dude, there's only one hotel in town. But Gordon Fall isn't staying with the below-the-line folks, you know?"

"Actually, no." My face scrunches up, and I glance at her with a wordless plea.

She quickly explains how film and television budgets are built and how key creative items go above the line, and technical items and crew positions go below the line. Staff who are above the line get individual title cards in the opening credits. Everybody else kinda falls into the category of plebes.

"Got it. Thanks for the crash course. If a

showrunner is above the line, where would Gordon Fall be staying?"

She sucks her cheeks in and rocks back and forth. "Like, I'm not supposed to know this, but I heard some scuttlebutt on set the other day. He rented Mitzy's dad's old crib. You remember Jacob Duncan's place, right?"

A faint image flashes to mind. "Barely. I got called out there once for a domestic disturbance when the place belonged to Cal Duncan, Mitzy's grandfather. Pretty sure I know the way. You'll set me straight if I make a wrong turn?"

"Totes."

Bristol rattles off directions, and eventually we approach a large granite stone bearing what I can only assume is the Duncan family crest with a large "D" in the center.

"Whoever bought this place didn't bother to change out the crest. That's strange."

Bristol nods. Her eyes are bright with anticipation, and she's biting her bottom lip unrelentingly.

"Are you okay?"

"Dude, I've never been here. Like, my mechanic buddy, Crank, drove me by a couple times when he was rooming with me. But, like, I never set foot on the actual property, you know?"

I'd forgotten what a fan girl she is. "You might

get the grand tour today. Do you know how to pick a lock?"

She puts her hands on her knees, pushes back against the seat, and *woots*. "Not like Mitzy, bro. She's next level, you know?"

"But you can do it?" I can't believe I'm encouraging a woman who could easily be my younger sister to behave like a juvenile delinquent.

"Totes. I got you."

Turning right, we pass through the massive wrought-iron gates and continue down the drive. And it is a drive, not a driveway. The house isn't visible as we curve gently through the thick birch trees.

The drive straightens, and an impressive mansion dominates the view. It sits on the shore of our vast great lake, but this massive home actually rivals the body of water.

The slate slabs of the driveway curve widely to the left, allowing room for fifteen to twenty cars to park in front of the three divided two-car garages. Two soaring gables sit astride a magnificent entrance, and autumn light spills through massive windows. The entire home is faced in split rock, and at least three chimneys poke through the steeply sloped roof. A terraced patio hugs the side of the home and works its way toward the surging waves. Definitely more than I remembered.

We both stare. Bristol gives a low whistle. "Dude!"

"I hear ya. Let's get after it."

I give the front door a formidable cop knock.

No answer.

There's a cyber truck in the driveway. "He's gotta be here, Bristol. Do your thing."

She drops to one knee and digs for the tools of her trade. She's nowhere near as polished as Mitzy, but what she lacks in skill, she makes up for in enthusiasm. "Dude, I hear someone screaming for help. You hear that, Mr. Harper?" She winks.

"I'm good with Erick. And yeah, I hear it too. That's probable cause in my book."

She goes to work, and I scan the grounds for anything unusual.

It takes Bristol three or four times as long as it would've taken Mitzy, but she gets us in.

"Now what?"

"Now, we hope he's fast asleep in his bed."

"Dude. Sweet."

"Stay behind me. If Gabby was having an affair with Gordon Fall and also knew dangerous secrets about him or the production company, we could be looking for a murderer."

"Like, I could take the upstairs while you check down here, boss." She beams eagerly.

Turning, I gaze at the woman who displays the

fearlessness of youth. "Bristol, did you hear what I said? Gordon Fall could be dangerous. You're unarmed. Stay behind me and have your phone ready. We might have to call this in."

"Copy that." She pulls out her mobile and holds it like a weapon.

With my gun aimed in the direction of advance, I tediously clear each room.

"Dude, how are there so many sets of steps on one floor?"

"Shhh." This is definitely Bristol's first search.

"Whoa! Look at that all that booze, bro." She tugs off her jester's beanie and presses her face against the curved glass doors that seal off the massive wine cellar.

"Interesting, but not what we're after. Stay close."

"Like, he's gotta be in the house, right?"

Continuing through the first floor, we find no sign of the Tansy Truth showrunner.

Heading up to the second level, we continue our hunt.

The first room we encounter is an opulent study, complete with coffered ceiling and a large bay window overlooking the lake. Towering waves crash against the shore.

Empty.

Five bedrooms and an enormous primary suite later, we still haven't discovered Gordon Fall.

Bristol points to the rumpled duvet and the open drawers in the primary bedroom. "Looks like he split, bro."

She's sharper than I imagined. Fact is, the evidence indicates someone hastily packed. "Well, his vehicle is out front. Maybe he called a taxi. That should be easy enough to trace."

"No doubt. No doubt." Her pom-poms sway with her motions.

"All signs are pointing to Gordon Fall strangling his mistress and making a run for it." I exhale in frustration. "Time to notify Paulsen and reach out to Eddie, my contact at the airport."

Bristol lifts and lowers on her toes as she waits for me to make the calls.

"Paulsen, we have a lead on the killer. Gordon Fall is missing, and it looks like he packed a bag. His vehicle's out front, so—"

"I'll take it from here, Harper. You really don't get how this works, do you? You're a civilian. You have no jurisdiction. You're a has-been. Take a powder and let the professionals handle this."

Without another word, I end the call, wondering if Paulsen felt all this animosity when she worked for me. If I'm fortunate enough to win the election, there's no way I can have her on the force in Pin Cherry. I'll have to transfer her. But where?

As Mitzy would say, that's a problem for future Erick.

"Bristol?" Where did she go?

"Just taking one more peek at the booze, bro." She snickers.

Gesturing toward the grand entrance, I motion for her to lead the way out. "Looks like he's on the run. The house is clear. Let's head back to set and see if anything has turned up. I'll call Eddie on the way."

"Noice."

CHAPTER 21
PYEWACKET

MR. HARPER PROMISED to escort me to the hospital. He has clearly chosen to shirk his duties. I haven't the time for these delays.

Mitzy needs me. This mess she's gotten herself into is beyond the talents of my dear friend Silas. It was never my intention to reveal my true power, but the balance between good and evil teeters on a razor's edge.

Mizithra Achelois Moon can tip the scales in favor of good. I must make it so.

Leaping from atop the great wardrobe in the apartment, still thankfully hidden from this mass of Hollywood vermin, I dart into the closet. I disappear into my warren of tunnels tucked between the vintage Chanel and the custom Vera Wang.

Emerging from the ventilation shaft within Mitzy and Erick's home, I locate the service animal vest discarded near the front door. It is beneath me to roll about like an inexperienced kitten, but without my long-lost opposable thumbs, extreme measures must be taken. After a mortifying struggle, I have donned the vest. My humiliation shall be the ticket into room 327.

It is a simple matter to gain access to the exterior. My warren has multiple entrances and exits. One must take great care not to be trapped by one's own cleverness.

I could've chosen any animal form I wished when I slipped away from Oberon. Real or fantastical. I toyed with the form of a centaur for a decade, relished the power of a dragon for a century, and discovered the perfect form only to miscalculate my spell work and arrive as a caracal kitten rather than a full-grown beast of power.

Isadora may never know how deeply she affected the rhythms of power in the universe when she rescued me from the clutches of that damnable animal poacher.

It feels magnificent to stretch my legs and breathe the crisp autumn air. The corridors of nature's wildness weave their way through Pin Cherry Harbor like no other place on earth. One can be in

the heart of the city, and yet bask in dappled sunlight beneath an ancient maple all at once. How
magnificent. How absolutely grand.

Emerging from the dying brambles across from
the medical facility, I inhale deeply and examine
the scents on the air.

My path is free of humans. It has been so for
three and a half minutes.

Lest I forget the age in which I now exist, I
glance up and down the street for the death machines these humans call cars. My safety is
confirmed.

Leaping across the thoroughfare, I dart between
careful clumps of landscaping and arrive upon the
mat outside the automatic doors.

Cautious, ever careful, I enter. Avoiding detec-
tion, I lurk under an abandoned gurney until the
elevator arrives.

With a quick flick of my tail, the doors open,
and the two occupants exit. No other life forms enter. Dashing into the elevator, I lift on my powerful
hind legs and depress the digit "3."

The doors close, and the lift inches me upward
to my destination.

This floor is amply staffed. Proceeding on the
necessary route without discovery seems hopeless.

Perhaps a distraction is in order.

With my mighty hind legs, I shove a food cart down the hallway. All nurses within visual radius gasp and run toward the trolley.

Through stealthy progression, I arrive at 327. Three is a magnificent number. It signifies creativity and often indicates a unique perspective, according to the ramblings of Pythagoras. The study of numerology, at the side of such a brilliant mathematician, provided hours of diversion in my youth.

Creeping forward, I nudge the door closed with my head before leaping onto the bed with Mitzy.

Her breathing remains steady. Pulse rate acceptable. Heart rate acceptable.

Why does she remain unconscious? Humans are entirely too fragile. This is the reason I chose to languish for over a thousand years, waxing and waning in the body of this feral feline. Each time growing stronger. Each trip gaining access to new powers and secrets.

Humans come and go. I've learned to avoid attachments. But despite my best efforts, Mitzy is dear to me. In all the eons of my life, none has provided more amusement, knowledge, or love.

Settling onto her chest, I press my nose against hers and begin the careful process of metering milligrams of my life force into her.

It is a finicky juggling act. If I release too much,

I will overwhelm her delicate system and bring about the result I so desperately seek to avoid.

Of course, there is also the possibility I would leave myself vulnerable to permanent death. Something I have no wish to explore.

As I reach the end of my ministrations, the door flies open. I have no option but to bury my head and purr like a hapless, domesticated — cat. The word sours in my mouth.

"How on earth did you get in here? Mr. Pyewacket, that is your name, isn't it?"

Turning, I treat the head nurse to one of my most condescending gazes.

She chuckles. "Let's see what you've done."

The woman checks the machines, makes several unnecessary "hmmms," and accesses her tablet to update Mitzy's record.

A sudden gasp for air from my acolyte shifts the energy in the room.

The shocked nurse rudely shoves me aside to gain access to Mitzy's chest.

Rather than suffer any further indignity, I wriggle free of the hideous service vest and plant myself regally in the visitor's chair.

The nurse, momentarily preoccupied, does not take notice.

She waves various fingers in front of Mitzy's

face, double-checking her vitals and typing hasty notes into the brightly colored tablet.

At long last, the limitless, soft-grey orbs blink to life, and Mitzy's precious gaze falls on me.

"Pye? How did you get—" She closes her eyes, opens them anew, and exclaims, "Shoot! I definitely died."

The nurse fails to reassure Miss Moon and runs to fetch the doctor. Taking advantage of the nurse's absence, I lunge across the gap and place my front paws near to her face. Lowering my eyes level with hers, I offer a single phrase in her chosen language. "I assure you, you live."

This display sends her bolt upright in her bed, clutching her temples and shouting for her beloved Erick.

Fabulous. My work is done.

With a final wink, I leap from the chair and escape the unpleasant odors and incessant beeps of the hospital.

At this rate, I shall return to the bookshop, ensconced in luxury before anyone notes my absence. Racing from the hospital, I make haste toward the wild.

The screeching of brakes rockets my attention to the here and now.

A Model T. Ah, yes. The mentor must check on his protégé.

I revel in the shock working its way across the face of Silas Willoughby.

Vanishing into the wilderness, I leave him to connect the dots and see Mitzy the rest of the way home.

For one more day, evil has been kept at bay.

CHAPTER 22
MITZY – IN THE HERE AND NOW

THE SIGHT OF SILAS WILLOUGHBY shuffling through the door of my hospital room is *almost* the best thing that could be happening. Let's be honest, my first choice was Erick.

"Silas! I'm—"

"I thought as much. I had a brief encounter with Robin Pyewacket Goodfellow prior to his disappearance into the woodlands. What news?"

"What news? That's all you can say? I'm pretty sure I was on the other side of the veil! Now you want to make small talk?"

Silas scrapes back the chair next to my bed, sits calmly, and steeples his fingers. As he bounces his chin on the tips of his pointers, it becomes clear. No answers will be given.

"Fine. This is some type of lesson. All I can tell you is I was in a weird place. It started out all swirly and psychedelic, and then it turned into some dark, twisted nightmare with Rory Bombay pulling my marionette strings. Horrifying! By the time Pyewacket arrived, I was pretty sure I was dead."

Silas falls still as a mannequin, and his jowls give one final aftershock.

"Are you going to say something?"

He harrumphs. "May I offer my most sincere apology? Had I suspected that we would be interrupted, I never would've allowed you to place that ring on your finger. The dark magic Rory Bombay drew into that creation seeped through the protections I put in place when Erick crashed—"

"Oh, Erick! Silas, I can't find my phone. You have to call him. Right away!" My hands fruitlessly search the paper-thin hospital gown.

Silas removes a small flip phone from a hidden pocket and begins to tap out the digits of Erick's phone number.

"Silas! No speed dial? Seriously? At least put it on speaker!" My face feels flushed.

His thick eyebrows knit together, but he places the call on speaker.

"Harper, here. Do you have any news, Silas?"

"Erick, I woke up! How soon can you get here?"

Now my heart is racing for entirely different reasons.

Rather than an elated cheer, my big announcement is met with silence. "Erick, can you hear me? I'm awake."

"I heard you. Things have escalated. I need to stop—"

"Erick No Middle Name Harper! You better get your fine behind over to the hospital *tout de suite*. The mystery of who tried to electrocute the electrician can wait." I wish he could see my perfect pout.

Another voice bursts across the line. "Dude, they whacked Gabby."

"Who?"

"The costumer, bro. Strangled with her own merch. Cold."

"Bristol, why are you with Erick? What's going on?"

Erick's confident voice cuts through the fog. "I'll explain when I see you, Moon. We'll be at the hospital in less than five minutes."

The call ends. Silas carefully folds his phone, replaces it in his jacket, and leans back in his chair without a word.

"Silas, what aren't you telling me?"

"Mr. Harper and Miss Linahan have located

Opal Williams. She inherited an actual castle on native lands in the Hawk Island reservation."

The lingering fog of unconsciousness muddles the sentence. My brain swirls within patterns and fuzzy memories. A strong hand touches my arm. "Mizithra? Is everything all right?"

The voice seems so far away it's as though I'm underwater— "Silas! It was her. Opal Williams is the one who stole Rory's remains. I'm certain."

"How did you come to this deduction?"

"Some freaky fever dream. Or coma creation. I don't know. I can feel it in every fiber of my body. She grabbed Bombay. Why?"

My wise mentor strokes his thick mustache, and his milky-blue eyes gaze into the great beyond. "She is no magic user. Inexperience or desperation led her to sell some of the most powerful items in Mr. Bombay's collection. There would be no reason to dig up the man's body—"

"Wait! In one of the visions or nightmares, or whatever it was, Rory mentioned the Oracle of Return. Maybe she's trying to bring him back!"

A calm hand cups mine. Soothing energy flows up my arm and fans out through my body. "You've had an enormous energetic shock to your system. It effectively overloaded your circuits. You were not dead, but you were in a type of psychic prison. Anything that you saw or heard was the creation of your mind. Neither Miss Williams nor Mr. Bombay had knowledge of the Oracle of Return. Your fear and worry created this false memory."

"But it seemed so real. I felt his creepy presence. I was wearing that stupid charm bracelet—"

"A carefully constructed ruse, created by your own dark thoughts. Mr. Bombay had no plan. It was clear from the moment you channeled his spirit. He was shocked that anyone remembered he had ever existed. There was no grand scheme. We all allowed our fears to manifest a problem that did not exist. I believe Mr. Harper is correct—"

The door bursts open, and Erick is across the room in two strides. His strong arms encircle me and his welcome woodsy-citrus scent is home.

"I missed you, Harper."

"I love you, Moon."

YOU MAY HAVE GROWN UP hearing the phrase nothing good happens after midnight. I'm not entirely sure I believe that, but I know for a fact that nothing good happens on an empty stomach. Thankfully, the first place Erick takes me is Myrtle's Diner. Bristol is "stoked" to ride in Mr. Willoughby's Model T, so the four of us meet at the diner and grab the corner booth.

Much to my delight, Odell is manning the grill

today. I'm warming up to the idea of his retirement, but nothing makes me happier than seeing his grizzled face and all-business buzz cut through that orders-up window.

"Why on earth would Rory Bombay leave his fortune and all of his questionable artifacts to a woman with no magical abilities?"

Silas harrumphs and smooths his bushy grey mustache with a thumb and forefinger.

Waving my hands in surrender, I attempt to right my wrong. "I know you take offense to the term magical, Silas, but it fits. Rory may have dabbled in alchemy, but he was no alchemist. He was way more interested in dark magic and anything that could be manipulated by spells or curses. The term works in this scenario. Would you not agree?" It secretly pleases me to use one of his nonsense phrases.

My mentor nods briefly.

Erick picks up the ball. "We can't be sure that's what happened. From what Grayskull told me, Opal moved pretty fast after Bombay's death. I wonder if all of that was above board?"

Bristol's eyes nearly pop out of her head, and her right hand taps a staccato rhythm on the silver-flecked white Formica table.

"Bristol, did you have something to add?"

"Like, when I was searching the web, you

know? I came across a bunch of questionable sales. Antiques and stuff that got sold on the cheap, bro. Super cheap even though they had a whole proverb, or whatevs."

"Provenance." Silas corrects her.

Erick turns toward me and arches one eyebrow. "Are you thinking what I'm thinking?"

Shrugging my shoulders, I reply, "Almost never. I'm thinking about how much longer until my french fries arrive. What were you thinking?"

He chuckles. "Yeah, I wasn't thinking about french fries. I'm thinking sweet little Opal Williams might be a forger. The fact that Bombay kept her on after Gershon, the original owner, died — he must've had a reason."

Smacking my hands on the table, I exhale loudly. "I urgently need to eat! None of my senses are working. Not the regular five and definitely not the extra ones. That totally makes sense, though." My stomach growls loudly.

Before I have a toddler-style meltdown, Odell arrives with our meals.

He wisely places my cheeseburger and fries in front of me before attending to his other patrons.

"Thanks, Gramps. You're the best."

"Glad to see you're back on the mend." Odell winks.

"Tally or Twiggy?"

"Hard to say. Gossip travels faster than wildfire around here." He delivers the remaining plates, rakes a hand through his mostly salt, but still a little pepper, buzz cut and grins. "Can you try to stay outta trouble until after the election?"

My mouth is full, but that rarely stops me. "Yeah. Can do."

Odell laughs out loud. A sound I've come to adore. Rough as a scouring pad but as comforting as a favorite flannel shirt. He raps his knuckles twice on the table and returns to the kitchen.

Taking a slug of soda, or, as locals call it, pop, I offer my two cents. "I say we head back out to Opal's castle and see what we can find."

Erick shakes his head. "We have no authority out there. If I talk Grayskull into getting us back into the castle, then what?"

"Maybe I can have a spell." I shrug my shoulders and look around for a better idea.

Silas scrunches up his face, and his hangdog jowls puff outward.

"Not like a magical spell, Silas. I meant a psychic episode. I can pretend to be channeling messages from the great beyond. Then, I'll use the ability you taught me about grabbing information from someone's mind — you know the one."

Silas shakes his head in frustration. "As clearly

as you've explained it, I'm surprised I have no recollection. If you are referring to the ability to perceive an answer that resides in a subject's mind, but remains unspoken, I am familiar."

Oh brother. "That's what I'm talking about. Anyway, I can pretend to be giving her messages from Rory, and maybe she'll slip up and think about the body. I'm telling you that vision I had about her stealing the remains . . . That's the only thing that seemed real in all the psychedelic nonsense I endured."

Silas steeples his fingers, and Bristol takes one look at him before turning to me with eyes as wide as saucers.

"Hey, Bristol is getting the hang of things. Yes, it's a lesson, B. And I don't know what it's about."

Erick leans forward and glides his left thumb along his stubbled jawline. "I might be able to give it a guess. You just got out of the hospital. You're definitely not at a hundred percent, and Silas is concerned about you launching into another psychic performance without proper rest."

A tender, weary expression graces my mentor's face.

Blowing a raspberry, I lean forward. "Look, the two of you can argue about this after we catch the bad guys. Maybe Opal's not involved with anything that's happening on the set, but she's absolutely involved in this empty crypt nonsense. Let's tackle what we know. Take that one off the board, and then we can all focus on who killed Gabby, or, if it *was* Gordon Fall, then where the heck is Gordon Fall? Deal?"

Silas reaches into one of his pockets, retrieves a small green vial, and hands it across the table. "If you are determined to move forward against my advice, at least take this."

"All right. Thank you. Am I using it now or do I save it for some situation down the road?"

Silas generally prefers I deduce everything on my own, but it is a testament to his concern for me that he provides an answer, rather than another lesson. "You may take it now. I believe it will assist in your recovery."

"Got it." Loosening the small cap, I refuse to inhale. If history has taught me anything, this concoction will not smell pleasant. Best thing I can do is toss it down the hatch before I lose my nerve.

The liquid in the green vial is indeed unpleasant. Actually, *unpleasant* barely begins to describe the noxious flavor. I swallow it as quickly as I can and fight my gag reflex. Within seconds, energy hums through my veins, and I can almost feel my cells being re-energized.

"I'm good. Harper and Moon are on the case,

right?" I give the group an enthusiastic "thumbs up."

Glancing around the table, I note three concerned expressions. Even Bristol isn't buying my act.

CHAPTER 23
MITZY

AFTER BRISTOL FAILS to convince us to take the "sweet" Model T, we load up in Twiggy's GMC and head toward the Hawk Island reservation.

When Erick and I walk through the door of the tribal police office, the genial round-faced man who greets us seems unsurprised by our arrival.

"I was pretty sure I had not seen the last of you, eh?" He shakes Erick's hand and turns to me. "And this must be your better half?"

I grip his outstretched hand and nod. "You're absolutely correct. I'm Mitzy Moon, and you must be the chief of police, Chief Grayskull, is it?"

He shakes my hand vigorously and makes a sound of agreement. "Glad to see you back on your feet. I could tell this one was awful worried." He juts his thumb toward Erick.

Erick prepped me on the way over, so I keep all of my *He-Man and the Masters of the Universe* jokes to myself. It's difficult, but I've matured since my arrival in Pin Cherry Harbor.

"Thank you. We were hoping — well, I was hoping — that you could take us out to see Opal Williams. I have some information that Erick wasn't privy to on his last visit. I might be able to make a little more headway. And there's a pretty good-sized possibility that you could make a nice arrest, if I'm correct."

Grayskull glances at the three officers pretending to busy themselves at their desks.

"Sayers, Mukwa, load up."

Grayskull waits patiently for the two officers to gather their gear and head out to a cruiser.

He spins his keys on his index finger. "We can take my car."

"Actually, we have a couple more people in our vehicle, so can we just convoy?" I shrug and offer a half smile.

Grayskull tilts his head at me, and amusement tugs the corner of his lip upward. "A show of force. That may not get us the red carpet, but it is bound to make her curious. Once that drawbridge drops—" He nods as though I've come up with a brilliant strategy.

Glancing from the chief of police to my husband and back, I swallow hard. "You weren't kidding about the castle? When you say drawbridge, you mean an actual—"

The two men nod in unison.

I can't contain my scoff. "Wow. Rory Bombay thought pretty highly of himself."

Grayskull snickers, and the three of us head out of the station.

The vehicles pull away from the tribal police station. Chief Grayskull leads the way, Erick takes second in line, and the two officers bring up the rear.

As Grayskull speaks into the security panel, I lean into my psychically enhanced hearing and report to the occupants of our vehicle. "The security guy doesn't want to let us in. Grayskull is playing tough. He pulled the, 'You are guests on this land. Your lease can be revoked' card."

Soon, the clackety-clack of the drawbridge lowering makes it clear Grayskull was successful.

As we drive across, I peer out the window and shake my head. "An actual moat. Wow! Just when I thought Rory Bombay couldn't get any more pompous or narcissistic. I can't believe he thought I would live here."

Erick seems to choke on his words as he grips the steering wheel with both hands. His knuckles whiten when he asks, "What are you talking about? When were you meant to live here?"

"Oh, it was one of those coma things. Probably not even true. Who knows?"

My flippant answer does little to calm my husband's nerves. I fear for Twiggy's steering wheel as his grip threatens to snap it in half. Plus, I fear a little for me, if I have to break the news to her.

"Harper, Bombay is dead. He's not behind anything that's going on here. He's impotent. Deceased. Out of our lives forever."

Erick's hands release their stranglehold on the steering wheel, and I can sense a flicker of relief swirling up his arms.

When the vehicle stops in the castle courtyard, Bristol is the first one out.

Erick tries to get her back in the vehicle, but she shakes her pom-poms severely.

"Dude, I gotta see the inside of this castle. Don't break my heart, bro."

Silas smooths his mustache and nods. "There's no harm in all of us entering. If you and Mitzy wish to speak to Miss Williams privately, I'm sure Bristol and I can entertain ourselves."

Leaning toward my mentor I whisper, "Is that code for give you a chance to search the place?"

He sniffs sharply and attempts to look indignant, but the twinkle in his eye tells me I'm correct.

Bristol leads the way to the massive double front doors, while I survey what could've been my prison if things had turned out differently. An involuntary shudder sends chill bumps down my arms.

Deep breath. Here and now.

Grayskull has a brief yet heated discussion with security personnel, and eventually the five of us enter. His two backup officers remain in their cruiser.

Opal descends an enormous mahogany curved staircase in a blood-red satin dressing gown, complete with ostrich feather trim. "Good afternoon. To what do I owe the pleasure of this return visit?"

Huh. Everything does sound friendlier with that southern accent.

Erick takes the lead. "Good afternoon, Miss Williams. As you can see, we were fortunate that Mitzy regained consciousness. Especially since you didn't have anything to help us. Funny thing is, she has some interesting information. Seems as though she may have received a message from Rory Bombay's spirit when she was in that in-between place."

Smart girl that I am, I kicked my extrasensory perceptions into overdrive before we walked in. I've left everything wide open and plan on focusing all of my attention on our hostess. The weird thing is, she's keeping her cool. Although the security guy by the front door is having a mini panic attack. Internally. Externally, he's a statue.

"Won't y'all join me in the parlor for re-freshments?"

She leads us into a room to the right where huge beams arch overhead and a roaring fire greets us. A polished silver tray supports a pitcher of iced tea with beads of condensation dripping down its curved side and six glasses. A veritable mountain of cucumber sandwiches languishes beside the tea.

It's almost as though our hostess had advanced warning of our arrival.

Opal takes a seat on a lovely blue brocade, high-backed antique chair. I'm sure she could recite its provenance, if pressed, while the four of us settle onto the spacious divan.

Grayskull paces by the fire.

"Can I get you anything, Chief Grayskull?"

"No thank you, ma'am."

His constant motion upsets her delicate sensi-bilities, but she does everything in her power to re-main calm.

"Miss Moon, is it?"

"Actually, it's Mrs. Moon. I kept my maiden name."

"Oh, how lovely. Modern girls and their inde-pendence."

Her response is absolutely an insult, but in that sugarcoated twang, it takes a true psychic to tell the difference.

"Thank you for saying that. Thing is, I was wondering if you could tell me what business you had with Rory Bombay's remains?"

The truth flashes through her mind for a split second. I barely have a chance to grasp it. The words that come out of her mouth tell quite a different tale. "I beg your pardon? I would have no use for them. I'm devastated by the news that they're missing."

She is a consummate actress. Maybe I can get her a role on the Tansy Truth production. "Interesting. It was my understanding that it was tied to a vault you discovered on these premises."

All eyes turn toward me.

The largest and most surprised pair belonging to Opal Williams.

"Did you need to put the remains in the vault?"

On cue, the answer flashes in her mind for an instant before she speaks her lie. "Again, Mrs. Moon, I haven't got the foggiest notion to what you are referring. I did everything I could for Mr. Bombay. He had no family to speak of, bless his soul. I made sure he was given a send-off fit for a king."

Shifting my attention to Silas, I pose a question. "Why would someone need a corpse to open a lock? Thoughts, Mr. Willoughby?"

Silas harrumphs, smooths his mustache with a thumb and forefinger, and nods once. "Perhaps you should call your stepbrother's girlfriend, Mizithra. I believe her name was Yolonda Olson. She was whip-smart. An inventor of some sort. Isn't she at MIT?"

Whipping out my phone, I quickly locate Yolonda "Yolo" Olson's phone number and am pleased when she answers on the first ring. "Mitzy! Awesome! Are you in town?"

"Not exactly. I'm not the kind of person MIT wants on their campus. Um, I'm in the middle of an investigation and I need some information. Got a minute?"

Opal Williams squirms in her overstuffed velvet chair.

"For you? Totes. What's up?"

"Why would someone need a corpse to open a vault?"

She squeals with joy. "Biometrics! You know this is, like, my specialty, right?"

"I didn't. But I know you're a genius, so I thought I'd roll the dice." Yolo and my stepbrother, Stellen Jablonski, are two of the smartest people I've ever met. They were a gigantic help on a strange case I handled a few years ago with a disappearing dog and an angry spirit. But that's another story.

"All right. What's biometrics? And explain it to me like I'm a toddler."

Yolo explains, in layman's terms, how fingerprints and DNA locks are part of cutting-edge biometric security.

"All right, but Rory's been in a crypt for a couple of years. How can you get fingerprints?"

Williams wants to crawl directly out of her skin at this point. I'm enjoying it all a bit too much.

Yolo carefully explains the process of embalming, the delayed decomp, and the rehydration of fingerprints with Rüffer's solution. The more excited she gets, the faster she talks. I get about half of what she's saying, but it's enough.

"That's amazing. You can rehydrate the finger and actually get a fingerprint that could open a biometric lock?"

"I've done it. The DNA lock tech, on the other hand, is super new. That would be way more complicated, and not commercially available. But I've seen crazier stuff. I'd go with the fingerprint angle first."

"Thanks, Yolo. You're a lifesaver."

"Ditto. And Bricklin says hi." A dog yodels in the background, and I can picture the adorable basenji lifting his pointed nose in the air to greet me.

I offer greetings to her precious pupper, and we end the phone call.

"Chief Grayskull, we need to search the premises."

At the mention of the search, Opal's carefully constructed defenses evaporate. I get all the information I need to help the team in their search.

Grayskull jumps on his radio and instructs his officers to come inside and assist with the search. Erick offers to stay upstairs and keep an eye on Opal and her security guards.

Knowing what we may encounter, I ask Silas to accompany us. And then there's Bristol. Cerberus himself could not keep her from joining our search.

Opal reluctantly directs us to the keep's basement entrance, and the six of us descend the stairs of hewn granite slabs that lead deeper and deeper into the dark and eerily silent below-ground level.

CHAPTER 24
MITZY

WHEN THE FIRST of the motion-activated LED torches bursts into fake flame, my hair wants to leap off my skull.

Silas places a calming hand on my arm, and we continue quietly to a large open area at the bottom of the steps.

Grayskull evaluates the three directional options before us, and I'm sure he plans on sending an officer down each tunnel.

We don't have that kind of time. "If I could offer some assistance, I believe our best option is the tunnel to the left."

He grins with understanding, and I feel as though he's peered behind my thin curtain of protection.

"Good suggestion, Mrs. Moon." Turning to his

officers, he delivers orders. "Sayers, remain here in case any of her employees attempt to follow."

"Mukwa, the rest of you, with me."

As we move down the hallway, my psychic senses take a barrage of hits.

The first is a clairaudient message. Simply Rory Bombay's name whispered on a loop, giving me the heebie-jeebies. The next hit begins with an icy circle swirling around the ring finger on my left hand. Glancing into the smoky cabochon of my mood ring, there's a vision, which I hope is entirely untrue. Finally, my shoulders tense with the sensation of deception, manipulation, and a soupçon of desperation.

Recklessly pushing in front of Grayskull, I steer the search to an iron door on our left. There's a lock. Lucky for us, it's not engaged. Opening the door, I gasp and throw myself backward. The vision in my ring was all too accurate. I'll spare you the gruesome details, but we have indeed discovered Rory Bombay's remains, and it appears Opal Williams has been hard at work rehydrating his fingerprints.

Grayskull steps in front of me and shakes his head in horror. "Why? Why in all of Mother Earth?"

He continues to wag his head in dismay as he holds the door, and our group moves into the room. The only one among us *not* horrified is Bristol.

"Dude! Your girl Yolo was, like, dead on. That's a whack contraption, though. Look." She steps closer to the suspended corpse. "That hand is, like, fully hydrated." Her eager expression pulls in the rest of us. "Where's this vault? Cuz, we're about to pop it open, bro!"

Silas and I share a moment of discomfort, to put it mildly, before Grayskull resumes command.

"I did not catch the young lady's name, but I believe she has the right idea. Mukwa, how do we wheel this thing down the hallway?" Grayskull steps aside and gives his officer access, then his eyes land on me. "Mrs. Moon, you seem to have an un-canny knack for treasure hunts. Any idea about the location of the vault?"

Despite the circumstances, I close my eyes and take a deep breath. The pungent, slightly sweet scent of the Rüffer's solution in the rehydration tank threatens to break my concentration, but I hold on by a thread.

"It's located at the end of the central tunnel. We'll have to roll him—" I swallow the bile rising in my throat "—all the way back there."

Officer Mukwa and Chief Grayskull take charge of the behemoth aquarium on wheels, while Silas scrapes the enormous iron door fully open.

Bristol hangs back. "I'll bring up the rear, bro. I got mad reflexes."

The police officers appear to have no idea what she's saying, but they don't disagree.

I lead the way, and, as we approach the open area at the bottom of the staircase where we left Sayers, I offer a warning. "You're about to see some real weird stuff. If you have a weak stomach, now's the time to look away."

The proud officer squares her shoulders. "I'm a hunter, the provider for my family. I'm strong."

"Suit yourself."

As the water tank on wheels emerges from the tunnel, I watch her strong shoulders quiver and the color drain from her face. To her credit, she holds it together, but — barely.

Grayskull instructs her to head upstairs and arrest Opal Williams for crimes against the dead and desecration of a grave. As Sayers turns, Grayskull adds, "And burglary, since she must have entered that mausoleum."

"10-4." Sayers departs with haste and does not look back.

Silas and I are forced to help redirect the unwieldy contraption to the central hallway.

Less than two minutes after Officer Sayers disappeared upstairs, my husband comes thundering down. "What in the—?"

Looking at him with a sickened expression, I

press my hand to my stomach and struggle to swallow. "I know, right?"

When we reach the vault, there seems to be no way to open the door. No handle, no crank, and no keypad. How did Opal find this thing?

Silas steps forward, moving his timeworn hands over the rusticated stone. He stops and depresses one of the rectangles.

The stone fascia lifts and slides into the wall as an oblong screen emerges. My mentor turns to the strangely constructed tank, holding the corpse in the Rüffer's solution, and examines the construction — including all available levers.

Opal must have stumbled upon this panel. Explains why she went after the remains . . . but ewww.

After careful consideration, Silas presses three in a particular sequence, draining the hydration fluid from the chamber supporting Rory Bombay's arm and hand. Next, he reaches into a compartment below the tank and dons thick rubber gloves. He then places the rehydrated hand on the screen. Several lights blink in sequence and there's a hollow note. Ping. Ping. Ping. Finally, a green light bar moves from top to bottom and scans the hand.

A negative beeping occurs, and Silas presses the hand more firmly to the glass.

This initiates a second series of pings and another scan.

It works. A green light illuminates.

Fingers crossed, that means success.

As the thick stone door shifts forward and slides open, images of two grips opening the crypt creep to mind. What have we done? Are we unleashing some evil? Maybe we should've done more to prepare.

When I survey my cohorts, I note that one of us is indeed prepared. My mentor grasps a thin red vial in his hand. It reminds me of a test tube from high school chemistry. To be clear, the energy I'm picking up is more deadly than any simple vinegar and baking soda experiment.

Bristol gasps and stumbles backward as a ring of LED torches bursts to life within the vault.

Erick pulls his weapon and follows Grayskull into the space.

With trained precision, the two men clear the vault. As they circle back toward the entrance, my eye catches something on the floor.

I step forward, but Silas grabs my shoulder and pulls me back. "The visions you experienced while in the coma have been too accurate, Mizithra. I fear this was indeed a prison built for you."

Clammy sweat forms on my palms, and I cling

to the familiar, fusty tweed coat as I call out, "Erick, what is that in the middle?"

Grayskull turns to cover him as Erick retrieves an envelope from the floor.

The muscles in my husband's jaw clench, and silent rage emanates from every cell in his body.

"What is it?" I lean forward as far as Silas will allow.

Harper holds up the envelope, and it looks to be addressed to me. Apparently by the same monks who illuminated the manuscripts in Ireland. Without the assistance of my psychic abilities, I doubt I would've deciphered the elegant calligraphy so easily.

Silas interjects. "Mr. Harper. It would be most prudent if you were to open the missive. I have countermeasures at the ready." His gnarled fingers raise the red vial a fraction of an inch.

Erick lifts the flap of the envelope, slides out a single square of parchment, and reads aloud.

"Dearest Mitzy,

"Happy anniversary, my darling. Do you like your gift? I had this built as a special anniversary surprise for you. Now we can fill this lovely space with all the powerful treasures this world has to offer. You are the vessel I've dreamt of all my life.

"Your loving husband, Rory."

Erick moves to tear the card in half. Silas jumps

in. "Please, Mr. Harper. It is of more use to me intact. There's something inexplicable in this vault. And if I'm correct, its purpose is to trap one particular person. I must examine that card, if I am to conclude the handling of this incident."

I wish Silas would speak more plainly, but, deep in my psychic heart, I know he's choosing his words with care in an attempt to tread lightly around the chief of tribal police.

Erick grumbles through his clenched jaw. "Only because I respect you, Silas." He shoves the card back into the envelope and walks toward the door.

Grayskull continues to scan the bare walls as he walks backward, covering Erick until they both exit the vault safely.

Erick hands the envelope to Mr. Willoughby, and my mentor carefully examines the creepy card.

Silas, ever the curious alchemist, must complete his experiment. "Mizithra, would you be so kind as to set one foot into the vault? Be prepared to extract it rapidly."

"Seriously?" Despite the current intensity, I can't suppress a snicker. "Silas, are you telling me to put one foot in and take one foot out? Then do you want me to 'shake it all about'?"

My joke lands with Grayskull. But he and I are

the only ones chuckling at my "Hokey Pokey" callback.

My husband steps behind me and firmly grasps my waist. "If she goes in, I go in."

Silas harrumphs, but he knows when he's been beaten.

With Erick holding me like a lifeline on a deep-sea dive, I extend my right foot into the vault.

In an instant, the huge door scrapes toward closure.

Erick yanks me backward, and Silas launches his red test tube into the vault.

"To the stairs!" he commands. With surprising speed, for his age, Silas leads the charge to safety.

A deafening crackle of electricity, followed by all sound being sucked from the air, swells in our wake. Wisps of blood-red smoke trail along the floor behind us.

"Faster, if you will." Silas picks up the pace, and we reach the stone stairs as the smoke recedes. "Chief Grayskull, perhaps you and your officer should check on Opal Williams. We'll seal up the basement and leave things in good order."

The police chief offers Silas a solemn nod, and he and Mukwa jog up the stairs to the ground floor.

As soon as they're out of earshot, I blurt, "Silas, did you break the spell?"

Silas offers an uncharacteristic chuckle. "An impossible feat without proper research. I simply sealed the vault. Permanently. Whether any future occupant possesses the fingerprints of Rory Bombay or not."

I'm about to offer my praise, when a sudden thought interrupts. "Wait! We have to go back and get that weird aquarium thing-y. Don't we need to return the body to the crypt?"

A sly grin lifts my mentor's ruddy jowls. "Perhaps I neglected to mention, anything touched by that smoke vanishes from existence."

"Dude, that's tight!" Bristol offers a slow clap. "Silas Willoughby for the win, bro."

Never a prideful man, Silas takes it all in stride. However, he can still catch me off guard. "Perhaps we can obtain another portion of those cheesed puffs as a form of celebration?"

The image of his orange-powder-covered fingers and mustache brings a welcome guffaw.

Erick, at last confident the worst is over, joins in my laughter. "I don't know what we're laughing about, but if that smoke means I never again have to deal with Rory Bombay — dead or alive — I'm all for it."

The four of us traipse up to the main floor, arriving as Sayers and Mukwa lead Opal Williams to a squad car.

Her sputtering protests are heartbreakingly pathetic.

"I didn't mean any harm. You have to understand, darling. I was so careful. Mr. Bombay was a beautiful man. I gave him everything. My loyalty, my heart, my deepest love. It was never enough. He was obsessed with her!" She jabs a perfectly manicured red nail in my direction.

"Oh, I didn't return the emotion, Opal. He's all yours."

She scoffs. "I only wanted to see what was in the vault. I couldn't bear to dismember him, so I brought the whole body. I intended to return it! If that Yankee producer would've kept to the agreed upon timeline . . . I swear to y'all I would've had everything neat as a pin. No harm, no foul. It's not really a crime now, is it?"

She continues her soliloquy, but I've heard all I care to. I tilt my head and smile at Opal. "Never trust a Hollywood producer, darling." Turning to my cohorts, I announce, "At least we know who gave the production permission to open the crypt. Seems like she put the nail in her own coffin on that one."

Bristol is the only one who giggles.

With a shrug, I change tactics. "Do you think she was under a spell, Silas?"

He shakes his head vigorously. "Not likely. Her

obsession seems entirely of her own making. Now, the hour is late and we must all recuperate."

And as though his words carry supernatural power, my knees turn to jelly at the mention of re-cuperation.

My handy husband scoops me into his arms long before there's any chance of me hitting the ground.

When I look into his loving blue eyes, a tear falls from his eye to my cheek. "Now this is the face I want to wake up to every morning. Don't you ever go getting yourself into a coma again. You hear me, Moon."

As I open my mouth to offer a witty retort, his lips are on mine, and everything else is forgotten.

CHAPTER 25
MITZY

As Erick drives toward Bell, Book & Candle, my heavy heart longs for the comfort of Grams and Pyewacket.

"How about we all head up to the old apartment, and I'll order Angelo and Vinci's? We can eat while we update the murder board."

Erick nods and, from the back seat, Bristol lets loose with a "Noice."

"I believe I shall take a rain check on your generous offer, Mizithra. I must return to my home and update my records."

Turning in my seat, I twist at an angle to get a better view of Silas. "What does that mean?"

"Much has transpired. It should be codified for posterity."

"Silas! English. Please."

He chuckles, smooths his mustache, and tries again. "Erick broke through a ring of protection, simply through the power of love. Rory Bombay created a trap triggered by a single energy signature. Yours. My counter-measure performed better than expected. However, I must update the calculations with precise impact area data, and I am in much need of rest."

"Whatever you say, Silas. If you want to miss the lasagna party, that's your call. Are you going to give me any explanation as to how and why Pyewacket spoke plain English to me?"

Silas fidgets, gazes out the window, and inhales sharply. "Perhaps this is more of the machinations of the coma. I would be hard-pressed to uncover any further explanation."

"Translation: you'll protect Pyewacket's secrets forever."

Silas folds his hands in his lap. "For as long as I draw breath on this plane."

A silent sadness descends, and the remainder of our drive to the bookshop is uninterrupted by conversation.

Silas takes his leave and shuffles off to his Model T, still parked at the diner.

The three of us enter through the alleyway door, expecting the hustle and bustle of the film crew.

The place appears deserted.

Concerned that more foul spells could be at play, I call out, "Twiggy? Are you here?"

My grumpy employee bursts from the back room, stomps toward me, and crushes me in an embrace. "Don't ever scare me like that again, kid."

"Copy that." I'm too shocked to say more.

Erick steps forward and says what I'm thinking. "What happened to the crew? You said you were looking at a twelve- or sixteen-hour day. If I'd known you needed your car. I would've—"

She waves her hands in surrender. "Simmer down. Gordon Fall never turned up. Shawna and that director guy — Noah, is it? Anyway, they had a shouting match, and she stormed off set. The camera folks shot some inserts, the lead actor's close-ups, and then called it a day."

My husband looks around the deserted set. "Well, again, if I'd known about the delay . . . Here are your keys, and I parked it pretty much where I found it."

She takes the keys and shoves them in the pocket of her faded dungarees. "Other than waking up Sleeping Beauty, did you guys find anything?"

Erick chuckles at the princess reference. "Actually, we're headed upstairs to update Isadora and Pyewacket. Mitzy's gonna call in an order to Angelo and Vinci's. You in?"

A strange expression flashes across Twiggy's face. It's an odd mixture of shock and sadness. "You guys inviting me into the Scooby Gang?"

Finally finding my voice, I step forward. "Twiggy, you've always been part of the gang. I'm sincerely sorry if I ever made you feel anything different. You're the most practical, logical member of the gang we have. I mean, you're pretty much our Velma!"

The cartoon reference tickles my volunteer employee. Her welcome cackle echoes off the tin-plated ceiling.

"I'm callin' in that order. You need anything special?" I arch an eyebrow in her direction.

She pats her chest as she catches her breath. "Get some extra garlic bread. And I wouldn't say no to a big slice of tiramisu."

"You got it." I point to Erick and Bristol in turn. "Lasagna and lasagna?"

They both nod. I fish around my pockets, and my eyes nearly pop out of my head. "Where did I leave my phone? Guys, I don't have a phone."

Erick swings a white plastic bag in front of me. "These are your personal effects from the hospital." Everyone shares a laugh at my expense.

"Oh, right." Pulling the bag open, I find my phone and a small mahogany ring box.

"How'd that get in there?" Reaching past the

phone, I grab the ring box and hand the bag back to Erick.

As I grip the lid, panic strikes me. Please don't be the cursed ring.

"My wedding ring! Silas must've put this in here when he — Never mind." I reach for the ring, but Erick beats me to it. He drops to one knee and extends the ring. "Mitzy Moon, I'd marry you every day if I could. How about you?"

Shoving my right ring finger through the ring, I follow through and encircle him in a hug nearly as tight as Twiggy's earlier embrace.

"Harper the Hero, I'm one hundred percent yours. No undead sorcerer is gonna swoop in and steal your gal."

Finally, everyone has a chuckle at someone else's expense: Rory Bombay and his delusional fantasies.

Tucked in the apartment, waiting for deliciousness to arrive, I reassure Grams. "I'm a hundred percent. I swear. All good. Silas approved." I gesture a "cross my heart" with one finger and offer an innocent smile.

"Pish tosh, young lady. You need rest. This murder board can wait. You need to send everyone home." She crosses her shimmering limbs and attempts a scowl.

Pyewacket emerges from the closet and backs

her up. "Ree-OW!" A warning punctuated by a threat.

Erick sighs and hangs his head.

"Hey, what's the deal, Harper? I'm good as new." Reaching out, I rub his back.

He twists toward me and sighs. "I can't tell you how grateful I am that you're safe. I gotta be honest, though, I was kind of enjoying hearing Isadora and understanding Pye."

Now I'm wondering if I'm still in a coma. "What the actual—?"

My sweet husband fills me in on the strange temporary powers he experienced, and Grams sighs with regret. "Just me an' you now, Mitzy. Girl power, right?"

Slipping into my side hustle as an afterlife interpreter, I share her thoughts with Erick and Bristol. "Yeah, girl power, Grams."

Eager to prove her worth, Bristol takes the baton and gives Grams all the dramatic details of their discovery of Gabby's body and the search of the old Duncan mansion. When she launches into the tale of our quest at the castle, my eyelids flutter and sag.

It's not until the BING BONG BING of the alley door buzzer startles me awake that I even realize I'd dozed off waiting for the food delivery.

Out of pure reflex, I shout, "He's here."

Grams giggles uncontrollably. She's the only

one who knows I'm referencing the good ol' days of Erick dropping by when we were dating. Everyone else assumes I'm excited about the food delivery. I mean, they're not wrong.

Erick kisses my cheek and points to the murder board. "We got everything handled. Are you sure you're not too tired? Maybe we can save dinner for breakfast."

Unable to stifle a huge yawn, I half-cover my mouth as I answer. "Let the record show, I accept his offer of sleeping rather than eating the world's best lasagna." With that announcement, I stumble back to the walk-up to crash out.

CHAPTER 26
MITZY

WHEN THE THIN FINGERS OF MORNING creep around the blackout blinds in the primary suite, I thank the powers that be for gifting me with a dreamless night's sleep. After everything I've been through in the last few days, I definitely needed a break from visions and premonitions.

Great. No sooner has the gratitude flowed through my mind than my fiendish feline leaps onto my duvet and drops a set of car keys.

Rubbing the sleep from my eyes, I glance at the pillow beside me and find it empty. The aroma of freshly brewed coffee wafts up the stairs, and I beam from the inside out.

"Robin Pyewacket Goodfellow, are you going to keep playing kitty cat? Silas wants me to believe that you speaking English to me was a hallucination brought on by my coma. Do you agree with him?"

"Reow." Can confirm.

"Fine. Keep your secrets, you little demon spawn." Reaching out, I pick up the keys and give them a once-over.

"These are the keys to Erick's Nova. Why would you bring them to me? You know he's not a fan of me driving his baby."

Pyewacket's powerful front paw swats the keys from my hand, and he pushes them back and forth, aiming the door key in the opposite direction of the trunk key. As I open my mouth to school him for his rude behavior, the word *trunk* whacks me upside the head like a wild pop fly in Little League.

"Gordon Fall isn't missing. He's in the trunk!"

"RE-OW!" Game on!

"Bristol said they searched the mansion. They never searched the trunk! And Erick said that Gordon Fall's car was—"

Racing down the stairs two at a time, I manage to make it to the first floor without breaking something.

Erick pauses, pancake in mid-flip, and scrunches up his face. "Are you late for something?"

"The trunk! We gotta go. There's no time for breakfast."

Erick holds the spatula like a weapon and narrows his gaze. "Stay where you are. Are you an alien? A trapped spirit? Where is my wife? There's no world in which Mitzy Moon skips dinner *and* breakfast."

Eager to convince him of my theory, I run through my conversation with Pyewacket and the situation with the keys.

"I can't argue with that logic, Moon. Meet me back down here in fifteen."

"Make it ten, and you got yourself a deal."

Mister "safety first" turns off the burner and meticulously covers the unused pancake batter. I have no time for such nonsense. Racing upstairs, I dress myself, scrape a comb through my haystack, and thunder right back down.

"Mitzy, where did you put those keys?"

"Keys?" What is he talking about?

"Moon, didn't you just give me a big speech about Pyewacket and my car keys?"

"Oh, those keys. I left them upstairs on the bed." I pat myself on the back for the great save.

He exhales and his shoulders sag, but as Erick heads for the steps, Mr. Cuddlekins prances down, holding the keys between his sharp fangs.

"Thanks, buddy." Erick bends and scratches firmly between Pye's tufted ears.

"Ree-ow." Soft but condescending.

Erick turns and his face falls. "Yeah, I can't understand him anymore. It was pretty sweet while it lasted. But I can't say I miss the thought dropping."

"You don't have to tell me! It's like the dream of showing up to school in your underwear." I roll my eyes and my lip twitches.

My perfectly formed husband scrunches up his pouty mouth. "I never had that dream. Weird. I did love talking to Pyewacket, though."

"Well, I'm back now. And I'll thank you to stay in your lane, Ricky."

THE TREES PART AND THE IMPRESSIVE MANSION GREETS US. Despite the bright sunlight and fast-moving clouds, the great lake is angry today. Huge waves crash against the shore, sending spray fifty feet into the air.

Erick and I exit the vehicle and take a moment to admire nature's spectacle.

"Now let's get into that trunk."

I head to the back of the dumpster fire of a vehicle. There's no lock to pick.

Luckily, my car-smart husband is a step ahead. He opens the trunk from inside the unsecured vehicle.

Even though I was expecting the contents, the shock is overwhelming. Covering my mouth, I turn away and struggle to get control of my stomach. No such luck. Running to the side of the enormous garage, I dry heave into a pile of fall leaves.

Erick calls from behind the vehicle. "You okay, Moon?"

"Yeah. I'm good. Probably should've had breakfast."

"Now that's the Mitzy Moon I married."

Refusing to take a second glance, I keep my distance. "What's the situation over there?"

He clears his throat. "Gordon Fall was literally stabbed in the back. Nothing special about the knife. Probably a weapon of opportunity taken from inside the house."

"When do you think it happened?"

"Hard to say. He went missing at least twenty-four hours ago. It's been unseasonably warm. He's been in the trunk — for a while. But based on what I'm seeing, he might've preceded Gabby in death. I'll call it in."

Despite my gurgling stomach, the thought of Erick sticking it to Paulsen yet again lifts my spirits. My inner child claps in delight as he places the call.

"Yeah, Paulsen, that's correct. Another body. Hey, it's not like I'm happy about it. Maybe if you were doing your job, I wouldn't have to."

Whoa. That one must have stung. I wish I could see her angry little face and watch her right hand squeezing the grip of her gun. Classic Paulsen maneuver.

"We could stay put until you get a deputy out here, but you may as well just send the medical examiner. Mitzy and I can stop by the station later and give our statements."

I like the sound of that.

"Suspects? You've crossed the line, Paulsen."

I don't like the sound of that.

Erick ends the call.

"What's going on? Who's a suspect?"

"She's accusing me of being the killer. Said it's too convenient that I've been the one to find all these bodies."

My chest tightens. "Do you think she plans to go public? We know it's not true, but the election is today!"

"Don't worry about it, Moon. I believe the citizens of Pin Cherry Harbor can recognize a scam when they see one."

"I admire your faith in humanity, Harper. I'm not so sure. We need to get back on that set and find out who the actual killer is — before Paulsen arrests you."

"She's not going to arrest me."

His desire to see the glass half-full would be adorable if it wasn't so delusional. "It wouldn't be the first time. She threw you in a holding cell when you were the *sheriff*. How do you think she'll treat you now?"

Erick's expression goes somber. "I see your point. We need to solve this case."

"Anything else you can tell me about the body? So I don't have to look." Erick takes a couple of pics, turns on his phone's flashlight, and searches the remainder of the trunk area.

"Nothing helpful. You want to close your eyes? I can guide you over here and you can see if you pick anything else up energetically."

"We don't have time. We have to get out of here before Paulsen arrives. Let's hit it, Clyde."

"You got shotgun, Bonnie?"

Amidst a sea of giggles, we hop into the Nova and burn rubber.

For the first time in days, the mood is carefree. My husband and I are cruising down the highway, on the way to grab chocolate croissants at Bless Choux patisserie. Plus, we're close to solving the case of the corpse in the costume trailer, and the specter of Rory Bombay has been permanently laid to rest.

Flashing lights on the road ahead bring a look of concern to Erick's handsome face. "Could be an accident. Should I turn around and take 131? It would add almost half an hour to the drive."

Squinting my eyes against the intense morning

sun, I peer at the scene. "I don't see any other cars. Just cruisers. No ambulance. No—"

"Is that SWAT?" Erick looks at me, and for the first time since I arrived in Pin Cherry Harbor, I wish with all my heart that I didn't have psychic abilities.

The sniper on the roof of the SWAT van takes aim. Harper slams on the brakes and jerks the vehicle to the side of the road.

He looks over his shoulder. "Are we being followed? Who are they aiming at?"

Reaching across the vehicle, I lay a hand on his knee. "You better place your hands on the dash and look as innocent as you can."

He follows my instructions, and I do the same. "Moon, what do you think is going on?"

"It's not what I *think*, Harper. It's what I know. My little joke has turned into a reality. That roadblock is for you."

He scoffs and removes his hands from the dashboard.

Paulsen's almost giddy voice blasts from a megaphone. "Hands where we can see 'em, Harper. Step out of the vehicle. Nice and slow."

Erick looks at me with a battle-hardened stare. "Are we doing this? Should we run?"

"What? You can't be serious! That's exactly what she's hoping you'll do. Get out of the vehicle, lay your firearm on the ground, and kick it toward her. Then we go quietly, and I call Silas."

His blue eyes darken with sorrow. "Mitzy, the election . . ."

The power-mad voice of Paulsen pierces the tension. "Step out of the vehicle or my sniper will fire."

When push comes to shove, I love to shove back.

CHAPTER 27
MITZY

WHIPPING THE DOOR OPEN, I hop out of the vehicle and walk straight toward Paulsen, running my mouth as I go. "You haven't got a shred of evidence to back any of this up. You may think this headline grab is going to save your career, but you just blew up your own campaign."

"Hands in the air."

As I scan the faces of the deputies manning the roadblock, it pleases me that none of them will make eye contact. They're doing the job the sheriff assigned to them, but it's clear they don't agree.

Closer inspection of the sniper positioned atop the SWAT van reveals the unmistakable blond locks of Boomer. If ever there was a guy that owed us a favor . . .

Erick slowly exits the vehicle. "I'm armed. I'm going to reach for my weapon, place it on the ground, and kick it toward you."

As though he never spoke, Paulsen shouts through her megaphone, "Drop the gun! Kick it toward me. On your knees. Hands behind your head."

She's enjoying this far too much. I'd love to experiment with one or two of my psychic abilities, but I can't take a chance on tripping her itchy trigger finger.

"Johnson, take Moon into custody."

Deputy Johnson shrugs helplessly and walks toward me. He doesn't even draw his weapon.

I offer him a knowing shrug and nod. He gingerly slips the handcuff over my left wrist, pulls it down, and clips the other cuff over my right. His voice is barely a whisper. "Sorry about this, Mrs. Moon. Are they too tight?"

"They're fine. You're just doing your job."

He escorts me to his cruiser and places a careful hand on my head as he tucks me into the back seat.

Paulsen takes no such precautions with my husband. She shoves him to the ground, sticks her knee in the middle of his back, and wrenches his arm down. My clairsentience tells me the handcuffs are biting into his flesh.

Yanking him to his feet, she shoves him toward her vehicle. I can hear the friction of her polyester pants reaching the ignition point as she marches forward.

It looks as though Erick's head encounters the vehicle as she crams him in the back seat without a care in the world.

Johnson didn't even take my phone. What a sweetheart.

Performing the alchemy Silas taught me for releasing handcuffs, I slip my wrists free and grab my phone. Johnson calls dispatch and reports he's en route to headquarters with suspect number two.

"Hey, Johnson, I don't want to startle you, but I'm calling my lawyer."

He nods. "Whatever you need to do, Mrs. Moon. This whole thing rubs me the wrong way. Not one deputy on the force believes that Erick Harper had anything to do with this. It's lazy police work. That's what it is. Please don't repeat that, Miss."

His secret is safe with me. "Silas, there's been an unfortunate turn of events. Can you please meet Erick and me at the sheriff's station? And if you can pull any strings regarding bail or release on our own recognizance, that would be great."

Silas harrumphs and tells me what he truly

thinks of Sheriff Paulsen before asking if I require sustenance.

"If you could bring us both breakfast from the diner, it would be much appreciated. We ran out of the house this morning without eating." His shock is audible.

"I know, right? We discovered the body of Gordon Fall in the trunk of his cyber truck. Maybe someone made a mistake and thought it was a dumpster, or maybe whoever stabbed him in the back was sending a message."

Silas is not amused by my cyber truck joke.

"Huh? No. I didn't get any *leads*. It might've happened in the morning, before Opal was taken into custody, so we can't rule her out. Yeah . . . or one of her henchmen. She doesn't seem like the type to damage her manicure."

Silas gives spontaneous advice on how to behave at the station.

"I won't say anything foolish. I'll ask Deputy Johnson to tell Erick. Thanks. You're a lifesaver, Silas."

Slipping my phone into my back pocket, I re-secure the handcuffs to ensure that Johnson receives no reprimand.

"Hey, I'm not sure if I'll see Erick at the station or not. Can you let him know Silas is on the way?"

"You got it, Mrs. Moon." He pulls into the parking

area behind the sheriff's station and turns off the engine. As he gently extracts me from the backseat, he offers another whispered message. "Just so you know, this isn't going to change my vote. I can't speak for all the citizens of Pin Cherry, but I vote with my heart. And I know Sheriff Harper, Mr.— Aw heck, I'm just going to say it. Sheriff Harper is the man for the job."

Flashing the best smile I can muster under the circumstances, I lower my voice and reply, "I appreciate the loyalty, Johnson. You're a hundred percent correct. Erick is innocent of these charges and he's absolutely the man for the job. I'm sorry I pulled him away from you guys for two years. Things couldn't have been easy under the rule of that tyrant."

Despite his efforts to remain professional, Deputy Johnson chuckles at the exact wrong moment. Paulsen has exited her vehicle and catches sight of the unauthorized mirth. "Something funny, Johnson? You want desk duty for the next month? There's a stack of cold cases that need to be alphabetized."

"No, sir. Sheriff. I am—"

"And take her phone, Johnson!"

Eager to come to his rescue, I jump in. "Don't worry, Paulsen. When the election results come in tonight, we'll all be laughing."

Her puffy face turns beet red, and unfortunately Erick takes the brunt of my inappropriate comment.

Note to self. Don't get sassy while husband is in handcuffs.

Paulsen takes Erick directly into her office while I'm placed in Interrogation Room One — minus my cell phone.

Wish I could say it was the first time I've been here, but I've managed to run afoul of the law more than once since I arrived in town. Plus, I helped on a few cases and got to come into this room as a *good girl*. Let's not forget about that.

Johnson leans across the hall and announces in a voice loud enough for me, Erick, and anyone in the bullpen to hear, "The suspect's lawyer is en route, Sheriff."

Paulsen slams something on her desk, probably her pudgy little fist. "What have I told you, Johnson? I'm running an interrogation here. There's no lawyer in sight. The suspect has been advised of his rights. He didn't ask for a lawyer. But now I can't question him, because you came in here and shot your mouth off."

"Sorry, Sheriff. I thought—"

"Do yourself a favor, Johnson. Don't think."

Johnson peeks his head around the door and

winks at me. I offer a grateful exhale and nod my head.

The cuffs are chafing, and I've had my fill of Paulsen's power trip. With a flash of concentration, I slip free of the manacles and place my hands on the table in front of me.

No one bursts into the room, so that tells me I'm not being observed through the one-way glass from the room situated between the two interrogation spaces.

Wow. I feel a bit ignored.

Paulsen's raised voice pierces the heavy door, but I'm proud to say there's nary a peep from my husband.

Silas Willoughby eventually arrives. He pops in to see me first, but I shake my head and point him directly to Erick.

Approximately fifteen minutes later, we're being led to a holding cell. Deputy Gilbert puts us both in the same cell. As he closes the door, he mumbles, "She said separate cells, but I don't hear so well these days."

Silas enters and passes our breakfasts through the bars.

While we eat, he fills us in on the situation. "She's charging you with everything she can scrape together. Sheriff Paulsen is even claiming you orchestrated a setup to impugn Opal Williams. I cannot be certain, but there's a chance she'll drop all the charges against Miss Williams. She plans to charge the two of you with all the crimes against Rory Bombay's missing remains. The sheriff shall levy murder one for Gabby and Gordon against Erick. Mitzy shall be charged as an accomplice. Of course, there will be attempted murder for the gaffer. I believe his name is Murray?"

Erick moans, and his head drops heavily into his hands.

I refuse to sit idle. "Silas, we need to get a statement to the press. This is ridiculous. Opal Williams is responsible for the theft of those remains, and we know exactly why."

Silas steeples his fingers and bounces his chin slowly on his pointers.

"Argh! Silas, I don't have time for a lesson. My brain is scrambled, my heart hurts, and I just need you to give it to me straight."

His hands drop heavily to his sides. "The facts can be interpreted in a number of ways. No one saw Opal and her crew removing the remains from the cemetery. We obtained that information from one of your . . ." He nods knowingly. "When we arrived at Opal's home, she claimed no knowledge. You are the one who led us to the chamber containing the remains — which are not in evidence — and subsequently to the vault. The only item in said vault was a letter addressed to you." He waves his hand and sniffs sharply. "Although, that letter has since vanished, but I'm sure you see the implication."

"By vanished, I'm sure you mean — Never mind. I get your point. There's no way Erick committed these murders. He was with Bristol at the time Gabby was strangled. And . . . well, he was pretty much with Bristol the whole day. When did he have time—?"

Silas harrumphs and wags his head slowly from side to side. "The time of death for Gabriella has been given as approximately 2:00 a.m. Mr. Harper has no alibi for that time. And because of the heat in the trunk, time of death for Gordon Fall remains undetermined."

He looks us over and continues, "The sheriff claims Mr. Harper killed Gabriella, then broke into the estate, murdered Gordon Fall, and hid him in the trunk of that vehicle."

Erick has reached his limit. He gets to his feet and slams one fist into the opposite palm. "What has gotten into her? We used to work together. Trust each other with our lives. How in the world can she think I would do this?"

Silas exhales with force. "Based on the statement she's making to reporters, she feels your time in the private sector has affected your judgment.

That perhaps your wife's misspent youth has led you astray."

Now it's my turn to stomp toward the bars. "Juvenile records are sealed! How did she—"

Silas waves his hand, giving us both the simmer down gesture. "All present know how effortless it is to access information in this day and age. I would be pleased to make a statement on your behalf, but I am afraid if any editors chose to print it, we could expect to find it buried on page ten. The headline will read, 'Former sheriff accused of multiple murders.'"

Erick collapses onto the steel bench. "Maybe she's right. Maybe I did lose my way. I let Bristol—"

"Please, Mr. Harper. Do not say anything here that you would not want on the record."

Erick glances left and right, discovering no invasion of privacy. "Those cameras are visual security only. When a suspect speaks with their counsel, there's no recording."

Silas lifts a thick eyebrow and tilts his head toward the camera. "Some things may have changed since your days as Sheriff, Mr. Harper."

My levelheaded husband slams his fist into the cinderblock wall, and bright-red spheres bubble to the surface of his knuckles.

Placing a hand on his shoulder, I gaze into his stormy eyes. "We can't let her get to us, Erick. We have to play it cool. Let Silas issue a statement. If they put it on page ten, so be it. At least it will be out there. If you remain silent . . . that's the worst thing we could do."

Silas verifies a couple of names and the time-line. He promises to return with supper and takes his leave.

CHAPTER 28
MITZY

"Now what, Harper?"

His expression is utter defeat. "Now? Nothing. I blew it. I rubbed her nose in it and she got the last laugh. This is not how I wanted to spend the election, Moon."

I feel like I'm tap dancing before the executioner. "Look on the bright side. You're still on the ballot. You haven't actually been charged with anything yet."

He shakes his hangdog head in silence.

Harper isn't going to help himself right now. It'll be up to me to get a message to Grams. There's clearly still a murderer on the loose.

There are only two people, one ghost, and one caracal who can track the murderer down while we're stuck inside.

As I place my hands on my knees and attempt to take a deep cleansing breath, a clacking on the wall behind me grabs my attention.

Holy *Little Rascals*. There's a string with a pencil and a piece of paper wrapped around it, being lowered through the bars of the holding cell window.

With no need for the help of my extrasensory perceptions, I know Bristol is on the other end of that string.

Sliding to the right, I rise and turn, hoping my body covers the item from the camera's view. Grabbing the string, I tug once, remove the pencil, and write my message. Securing the pencil and note to the string, I tug twice and wait for it to disappear through the bars.

Unfortunately, the pencil is turned the wrong way when it reaches the window.

"Erick, can you give me a boost?"

He glances at me, seemingly oblivious to the high-level spycraft happening around him.

"Moon, I love you, but you cannot fit through those bars."

"It's not me that's trying to fit, Harper." I tip my head toward the window and insist on a boost.

He rolls his eyes, locks his fingers together, and lifts me up.

Grabbing the pencil, I turn it and shove it through the bars.

A soft "Noice" reaches my ears as feet pad away down the alley.

"This is ridiculous! Paulsen hasn't charged us with anything, right? Why couldn't Silas just walk us out of here?"

"Paulsen can hold us for forty-eight hours. Then she'll have to charge us or release us. It may not be how we wanted to spend the election day, but here we are."

"You still have a decent chance, Erick. Voters will make the right choice."

Thoughts are clearly bouncing around in his head like a loose pinball. After careful consideration, which I feel certain Paulsen doesn't deserve, he replies, "She has a decent arrest record. It's a tough call."

I throw my hands in the air. "Of course she has a decent arrest record! She arrests everyone. The innocent. The guilty. We're proof of that!" Banging my fist against the iron bench, I wince in pain. "Ow! Ow. Ow. Ow."

Erick slides closer and gently massages my wounded hand.

The heavy steel door to the holding area slams open. A teenager snaps several pictures before identifying himself. "Jay Fellows, *Pin Cherry Harbor Post*. Any comment?"

Taking a deep breath, I fill my lungs with enough air for a massive rant. Before I can launch off the bench and tear into this clueless child, Erick hooks his hand through my elbow and gives me a gentle squeeze as he whispers, "Don't take the bait."

Remaining seated in silence is not how this was supposed to end. My insides feel like someone lit the fuse, and I'm helpless as I watch the sparks creep closer and closer to the TNT.

The kid shrugs when he receives no reply, swipes through the photos he took on his phone, and leaves.

As soon as the door latches . . . "Why wouldn't you let me say anything?"

Erick slips an arm around my shoulders and holds me close. "Think about it, Moon. He didn't get in here without permission. Paulsen, or an authorized deputy, had to unlock the door to the holding area. She wants us to say something — anything. And then she'll find a way to twist our words to match the agenda she's pushing." He sighs as he rests his elbows on his knees and stares at the bare concrete. "Let Silas handle it."

"I wish I'd never given Quincy Knudsen that journalism scholarship to Columbia! First of all, he would've taken a way better picture of me with his classic film camera, but the other thing is, Quince always got his facts straight. I can't believe the elder Knudsen would print a story without checking it. That newspaper has been in their family for generations. What is going on in this town?"

Erick, whom I'm now considering calling the Human Xanax, calmly replies, "Hey, even if they check the facts, they're gonna end up with the same headline. We are in jail. I am accused of murder. You are accused of being an accomplice. Those are the facts. You've heard me Mirandize suspects before, right?"

I feel like a teenager being outsmarted by a wily parent. "Yeah. Why?"

"Anything you say can and will be used against you, etc. It's better to keep your mouth shut in situations like these. Trust me."

Relenting at long last, I lay my head on his shoulder and blow a raspberry. "It's not fair. We could solve this murder in a flash. It's not fair."

Erick strokes my hair. "I agree. We have to trust that the people in our inner circle, people who believe in us, can carry the ball into the end zone. You said it yourself: Bristol is smarter than you gave her credit for. We both know Silas Willoughby always has a trick up his sleeve. Don't give up hope."

"Harper, do you trust me?"

My husband lifts his weary head and rubs one hand on the back of his neck. "With my life. Why?"

Slipping the lock pick and tension wrench from my pocket, I move toward the cell door. "I gave up my phone willingly. But they didn't ask for anything else."

Erick's eyes widen to saucers, and he hustles across the holding cell. "No. There's gotta be a better way."

Dropping my shoulders with a huff, I announce, "You're no fun."

He paces while I take three deep breaths and tap into my extrasensory abilities. When all else fails . . .

"Hey, we could solve this case, right?"

Erick tosses his hands in the air in frustration. "Yeah. If we weren't stuck in here."

"But we are stuck in here. Think about it. We basically have all the information we need. Let's just calmly review the case. There's gotta be something we missed."

His pacing abruptly stops. "Is Mitzy Moon the voice of reason right now?"

Kicking one heel up behind me, like a girl in a Rom-Com, I smirk and wink. "Anything's possible." Then I turn to the blank wall of the holding cell and curse under my breath. "I should've kept that pencil!"

CHAPTER 29

MITZY

Erick slips up behind me, scoops his arms around my waist, and kisses my cheek. "Nonsense. You've got a magic brain, Moon. We've got this."

I do love a sweet compliment. "All right. We know Opal Williams gave them permission to open the crypt. So why would she kill Gordon?"

My rational husband waves his hands in surrender. "Whoa. We don't have any proof Opal killed Gordon. Let's take that off the table."

"Fine." I plant my fist on my hip, and visions of Shawna Fenty come to mind. "What about that lead actress? She slept with Gordon to get the part, but the director hated her. Maybe in a fit of narcissistic rage, she killed Gordon?"

Erick eases back on the steel bench and crosses

his ankles as he laces his fingers together behind his head. "Maybe, but when she discovered Gabby's body, she came running in screaming for Gordon. Why would she do that if she'd already killed him?"

In case you're worried I forgot to sneak a peek at his lovely abs when his shirt hiked up, let me assure you, I did not. Now, back to business. "She's an actress, Harper. Maybe she was screaming for Gordon because she knew he was dead."

BRISTOL

Booking it down the alley away from the five-o, I toss the string and the pencil in a dumpster and read the note.

"Grams and Pye can help. Murray. Gabby. Gordon. Motive? Need proof. You'll figure it out. Counting on you. M&E."

"Noice. The boss knows I can handle my business."

The set is abandoned, and the bookshop is locked up tight. Pushing the service bell, I hope for triple cherries. Mama Linahan was a big gambler. I spent a lot of my half-pint days wandering around the casino, totally lone-wolfing it, you know? The door opens, like, a crack. Two huge golden eyes have a bead on me. "Dude! Is that you, Pye? Like, I didn't know you could open doors. Sweet, bro."

He leads me to the secret apartment, but I got no clue how the door works.

"Hey, Mitzy's grandma. If you can hear me, like, I can't open this thing."

The bookcase slides open, and I figure it must be the work of the ghost. Pyewacket leads me in, and I pin the note from Mitzy and Erick on the murder board.

Then I get super freaked when the pen on the coffee table starts moving. "Like, you're the ghost chick that writes messages and stuff, right?"

She floats me a question.

"Yeah, both Mitzy and Erick are locked up, you know."

It takes me a minute to refresh all the deets on what happened on the rez with Opal and that guy in the tank. But once I get the hang of this chat thing, she comes up with some sweet ideas. "Yeah, the place cleared out downstairs. Ghost town, bro. I mean, not like—"

She draws her version of the crying laughing emoji on a card. The next card says "Production trailer."

"Yeah, dude. I can pick that lock. Erick says I'm pretty good, bro."

MITZY

Erick gazes at the blank ceiling and blinks slowly. "What did you mean the director didn't want her?"

"Bristol told you what Gabby said, right? That Shawna slept with Gordon to get the part, but Noah Madson didn't want her."

"Right." He throws his feet off the bench and returns to a seated position. "But why would a producer cast a terrible actress?"

He has me stumped for a second. "Yeah. And he made a point of saying this was Noah's directorial debut. It's almost like —"

"Gordon was sabotaging the production!" we shout in unison.

I'm overcome with joy. Erick is more confused than ever.

"Why would anyone want to sabotage their own film, Moon?"

Now I'm pacing. "There's this thing, called — what is it? It's an extra expense . . . imminent peril insurance! It covers the production company if you have to shut down filming due to a disaster. It used to include pandemics until we actually had one." I wag my head and arch an eyebrow. "Thing is, those policies can be worth millions. Maybe Gordon Fall took one out on this project because he wanted it to fail. Maybe he was pushing it toward disaster!"

· · ·

BRISTOL

Pyewacket hangs with me when I head out to the alley to locate the production trailer. Takes me a couple minutes to pick the lock, but, you know, we get inside.

Scripts, schedules, empty coffee cups, an ash-tray piled with cigarette butts, and a binder with "Director's Notes" on the cover. "Must be Noah's desk, dude."

There's a laptop on the desk, under some papers, so I slide into the chair to work my magic.

"This is Gordon Fall's computer, bro. Why would Noah have it?"

Pye cops a squat next to me, so I spill the tea.

"Dude, there's a bunch of emails from Opal Williams. She's the one who gave the thumbs up to, like, crack the can on Rory, you know. They were paying her a fortune!"

"Reow." Can confirm.

"Sounds like a yes, bro. I got you."

"She was fighting with Gordon about the date, bro." I scan a few more. "Nothin'. We know all this."

Pye raises onto his hind legs, placing two paws on the desk.

"Bro. Look at this!" I point to the email and laugh. "Dude, I'm, like, talking to a cat."

A bunch of the emails are from some insurance

chick. All about imminent peril stuff. Covers the production if they shut down.

"Dude, what if the big dog, Fall, wanted to get shut down?"

"Reow." Can confirm.

MITZY

Erick gets to his feet and paces in the opposite direction. Each of us wearing a separate track across the small cell.

I'm on a roll. "All right. He casts a bad actress, hires an inexperienced director, and clearly hired the worst screenwriter he could find! I mean, that dialogue!"

He pauses, looks at me, and nods his agreement. "Now Gordon Fall is dead. How could he be responsible for sabotaging the production if he didn't survive long enough to collect?"

My mood tanks. "And how would killing Gabby sabotage the production? Gordon promoted her from the electric department to head costume—"

Erick grips my arm. "What did you say?"

"When I met her, she told me she'd gone to fashion design school but had to take a job in the electric department to get her foot in the film production door."

My husband grips both my shoulders and gazes

into my eyes. His gorgeous baby blues utterly distract me.

"Moon, focus up. Wasn't Gabby also sleeping with Gordon?"

"I don't know about *also*. But after, and currently. So yeah, whatever."

His eyes brighten. "So maybe she was helping him with the sabotage. Maybe she's responsible for electrocuting Murray."

Placing a hand on my forehead, I inhale sharply and feel the wheels in my brain turning into overdrive. "Ooooh. Her comment about knowing where the bodies were buried. Maybe it had to do with knowing about the sabotage. But then she messed up. Murray lived, and Gordon was worried she'd lose her nerve and rat him out."

Erick makes an entire lap around our small quarters. "Okay. Gordon strangles Gabby, and then what?"

I'm nodding. "Then he hurries back to the mansion to pack a bag and make a run for it?"

Harper collapses onto the steel bench. "But how does he collect the insurance money if he's on the run? Our motive just went up in smoke."

Sliding next to him, I place both hands on his left knee. "Not necessarily. Gordon's the executive producer. He could make up some excuse about having to hurry back to Hollywood to take a meeting or whatever. Then he could still shut down the production." Rubbing my hands together, I continue, "An attempted murder. Then an actual murder. That could be enough to force the disaster coverage to kick in."

Erick exhales as he leans against the back wall. "Okay. But he never made it. And his accomplice was already dead. So who killed Gordon?"

"Could it have been Opal's goons? She doesn't do her dirty work. Maybe she had one of her henchmen handle it."

He scrapes a loose swath of his blond bangs back and moans. "It doesn't make sense, Moon. Opal's crime was already exposed. Killing Gordon wouldn't get her anything, except a charge added to her list. It had to be somebody else."

"All right." I smack my lips together with a loud pop. "Jealousy, revenge, money. Who had the most to lose?"

Erick taps each of his fingers, perhaps silently ticking off a list of names in his head. "What about Shawna Fenty? This was her big break. If she found out Gordon was—"

"Have you seen her arms? She's basically an animated toothpick. She doesn't have the strength to move someone Gordon's size."

He slumps on the bench, and I slump beside him.

"We're running out of suspects. I mean, the only other person who had everything to lose was — the director!"

BRISTOL

"Now this Noah dude has Gordon's laptop. Know what I think, bro?"

The cat puts a heavy paw on my leg.

"This Noah dude smokes a lot." I point to the overflowing ashtray.

"Reow." Can confirm.

Pulling off my beanie, I stretch it to help me think. "Whoa! Dude, now that you mention it, like, I kinda smelled 'stale casino' out at the mansion, you know?"

Pye heads toward the door.

"Yeah, we solved it, bro."

As we walk down the alley, I remind myself to think like Mitzy. "Dude! That Noah guy is gonna, like, flee, you know?"

"Reow." Can confirm.

"Noice! I gotta call that dude Erick was talking about . . . Ernie? No. Eddie!"

MITZY

Erick's jaw clenches. "Did you say Noah was a smoker?"

"Yeah, but seems like he was trying to quit. I saw him pop that nicotine gum a few times. Why?"

"Thinking back, there was a faint tobacco odor at the mansion. And the suitcase was under the body. Like Gordon had packed it and then went back in to get something."

My heart is racing. It feels like we're on the right track. "Then Noah showed up and argued about the suspected sabotage. He grabbed a knife and stabbed him in the back in anger. The trunk was probably still open."

Erick bobs his head excitedly. "Right. Noah threw the body in. If he had packed the bag as an afterthought, it would've been on top of the body."

Gripping my husband's arm, my hands shake as I squeeze. "Erick, Noah Madson is probably flying out of town right now. We're the only ones who figured this out. Now, can I pick the lock?"

He shakes his head.

Marching straight to the bars, I bang against them and shout at the top of my lungs. "I need to call my lawyer! I'm entitled to a phone call!" Staring directly into the camera, I point my finger and shout, "Paulsen! Open this cell!"

CHAPTER 30
MITZY

"COME ON, MOON." Erick pats the bench beside him. "Try to get a little shut-eye. We'll need the strength when we have to face the election results in the morning. I'm hoping it's too close to call tonight. A guy can dream . . ."

"When I get out of here, I'm going to bring Paulsen up on charges of violating the Geneva Convention!" Dropping my hands to my sides in defeat, I shuffle toward the bench.

"That doesn't actually apply here." Erick chuckles softly, but the exhaustion is just beneath the surface.

After months of campaigning and spreading goodwill throughout the community, things literally couldn't have ended worse. I've worked so hard to shift my perspective since I arrived in almost-

Canada. To be grateful for what I have and to be kind. But this injustice makes me want to empty the coffers on a rampage of vengeance.

Long, sexy fingers flutter in front of my face. My cheeks flush red. "Yeah, mind movies. Budge up, Harper." I use one of my standard roller derby maneuvers, the hip check, to scoot him down the bench as I lay my head in his lap.

No sooner have I given up hope than the steel security door scrapes open.

I'm on my feet in a flash and press my face between the bars.

The cell door next to us opens and, to my shock, Deputy Johnson propels Noah Madson into holding.

"Johnson, what's going on? I need to call my lawyer. Can you get me out of here?" His head turns in my direction, but he doesn't make eye contact. "I'll run it by the sheriff, Miss."

He turns to exit.

"Johnson! Noah Madson is the killer. I'm sure of it. What are Erick and I still doing in here?"

With his back to me, Johnson shrugs and leaves the holding area.

Turning toward my cellmate, my face frozen in shock, I move my mouth, but no words escape.

Erick slides down the bench toward the other

holding cell. "Hey, Erick Harper here. What are you actually in for?"

Aha! Befriend the murderer. I hadn't thought of that. This is why we make such a good team. How am I going to run that agency on my own?

The deflated newbie director slowly swivels his head toward the question. "You want the real story?"

Since butting in is my specialty, I step toward the shared bars and arch one eyebrow. "I'd love nothing more. What happened?"

"My agent came across this project. This *Tansy Truth* script. She said the script was terrible, but the source material was brilliant. She claimed she could get me a deal to direct and co-write — that I could rewrite the script and create a masterpiece. She promised me indie production glory."

Erick and I nod, and I join my husband on the bench.

Noah rolls his head back and forth on his pudgy neck, as his sloped shoulders seem to hang even lower. "What was I thinking? I grew up in Hollywood. I went to USC. I've heard the stories my whole life, but when it happened to me, I couldn't see the forest for the trees." He scoffs openly.

I feel his pain. With what little experience I have, I know exactly how easy it is to fall under the spell. "It's not entirely your fault, Noah. Every agent and producer out there attends some special mind-control classes. I'm sure of it. They know exactly which words to use and which buttons to push to draw you into their web. What happened?"

He acknowledges my comment with a quick nod and continues. "Everything was going according to plan. Then the studio brought on Gordon Fall. That's when everything changed."

Erick and I make some guttural noises of agreement.

"He announced they were going with the original script. He said the source material wasn't up to snuff, and if we wanted an exclusive distribution deal with one of the top streaming services, we needed the mass appeal that the original adaptation provided." He stands and walks towards the bars. "You're the author, Mrs. Moon. Can you believe that?"

Not being the actual author, I imagine how my grandmother would feel and attempt to channel her. I mean, not *actually* channel her. I don't think I'll ever try that shtick again. "Honestly, no. I heard that stilted dialogue at the crypt. Wherever that scene came from, it was terrible."

Noah raises his hands in the air like an inspirational speaker revving up a crowd. "See? I knew it!" He paces. "Then we got to casting. Enter, Shawna Fenty. She was the last actress we saw at the end of the first day of auditions for the main character. By any stretch of the imagination, she was the worst."

I scoff and add, "Yeah, her and the lead actor didn't seem to have any chemistry."

He stops and turns. "Don't even get me started on that. Some underwear model turned actor. If we were filming the sequel to *50 Shades of Grey* . . . Never mind. He's got one look. Did you see it?"

Shades of *Zoolander* pop to mind. I can hear Will Ferrell uttering his famous line about crazy pills. "Yeah, he does *smolder* like a pro. But that's all he's got."

Noah approaches the bars and shows his hands to indicate he comes in peace. "Mrs. Moon, you get it. I know you're a wealthy woman. You could personally finance—"

"Let's cut ahead to the part where you murdered two people and attempted to kill another, Mr. Madson." Stepping back from the bars, I cross my arms over my chest and jut my chin toward him.

He waves his hands in surrender. "You got it all wrong. I didn't kill them. I mean, I'm responsible for Gordon, but hear me out."

I gesture toward him with a look that clearly says convince me.

Noah reveals the twisted trail that Erick and I had put together with shocking accuracy. Gordon's plan to sabotage the production and Gabby's blind assistance.

The young director sighs. "Gordon used Gabby to kill Sparky, Gilbert Murray. Murray's an astonishing lighting designer. Even with Shawna's terrible acting and the weak script, his lighting setups were going to save us. Gordon Fall couldn't have that."

Erick rises from the bench and steps toward the bars. "Mr. Madson, you're certain Gabby sabotaged the generator?"

"Absolutely! There's no one else who knows anything about generators. I mean, the guys in the electric department, but they would never cross Sparky. He always works with the same crew — a package deal. Those guys have tied their livelihood to him. No question. It had to be Gabby. And then, Gordon killed her."

Erick sniffs sharply. "You can prove this?"

"Those designer shoes that she was strangled with? They're not a wardrobe item. Those were a gift from Gordon. I went out there to confront him. To convince him to back off and support the project and save both our careers."

My turn. "How could you be sure Gordon wanted to sabotage the production? Maybe he's just a terrible producer. There are plenty of those." I offer a smug nod of my head.

Noah grips the bars pleadingly. "There are. I hear what you're saying. But I found the emails on his laptop. He was looking into triggering the imminent peril clause of our insurance coverage. Gordon told the insurance rep there'd been a murder on set. But that was before Gabby went down." He lifts one finger in the air and shakes it with conviction. "That's how I know she screwed up and that he owed them a murder. Gordan silenced the only person who knew about his plan and satisfied the insurance company in one fell swoop."

Erick and I exchange a knowing glance. "And what about Gordon? Who killed him?" Erick grabs the bars and stares daggers at Madson.

The broken man hangs his head and exhales volumes. "It was me. It's all a blur. I went out to the mansion to confront him face to face. He said the deed was done. All that remained was for him to cash the check. Then he walked away from me like I was nothing. I lost it." Noah rubs his hands across his balding head and groans. "I grabbed a knife from the block on the counter, and— Once I realized what I'd done, I had to cover my tracks. I thought I'd be long gone by the time anyone found his body."

"Yeah, so did we." Erick looks over his shoulder, and I hastily nod my agreement.

"So why are you not long gone, Noah?" I stand

beside my husband, and we both await an explanation that makes any kind of sense.

As Noah opens his mouth, the holding cell door blasts open. Deputy Gilbert walks in holding a newspaper.

He steps toward our cell and pushes it through the bars. I snatch it from his hands, clock the headline, and let it flutter to the floor.

Erick glances down and reads aloud. "Former Sheriff accused of multiple murders." He steps toward me and slips an arm around my shoulders. "We did the best we could, Moon. Thanks for standing by me."

Deputy Gilbert remains on the other side of the bars. He steps back, and I catch a flash of a grin before he gets it under control.

Strains of "For He's a Jolly Good Fellow" reach my ears, and Erick and I turn to see half the town squeezing through the security door behind Odell. In my grampa's hands, he holds a giant sheet cake bearing the message 'Congratulations, Sheriff'!

THE NEXT MORNING'S special edition of the *Pin Cherry Harbor Post* carries a photo of Sheriff Erick Harper in his freshly pressed uniform, holding a copy of the newspaper accusing him of murder. The edition had sold out before breakfast, but someone was kind enough to buy one for us and leave it in our mailbox.

When we arrive at the diner, the place is packed. Everyone gets to their feet and gives Erick a standing ovation. Odell offers a spatula salute through the orders-up window, and Ezra smiles warmly.

Despite the crowd, the corner booth stands empty. A handwritten "Reserved" sign sits atop the silver-flecked Formica.

Erick and I slide onto opposite red-vinyl

benches, as Tally hurries over with steaming mugs of black gold. "Congratulations, Sheriff Harper. Heard you solved two separate cases your first day on the job." She winks. "We never doubted you."

I thought I had no more tears of joy to cry, but all I can do is nod as I grab a thin paper napkin to dab at my eyes. Noah Madson is looking at life in prison, and expert forger Opal Williams can expect jail time and a hefty fine — thanks to the amazing power of teamwork.

Sheriff Harper, his voice choked with emotion, reaches out and shakes Tally's hand. "Thank you. Folks like you are the reason I ran for office." He snuffles and attempts to hide his emotion behind his mug of coffee.

Tally bobs her flame-red bun and rushes off to attend to her myriad customers.

Odell and Ezra march out together, each holding a separate plate.

Ezra slides my standard fare and a bottle of Tabasco in front of me. Odell places a mile-high stack of blueberry pancakes surrounded by sausage links in front of Erick. Then he snaps to the position of attention and pops a salute. "Welcome back, Sheriff."

Erick dips his head in that way that insinuates he's doffing a cap and chokes out a reply. "Thank you, sir."

Ezra returns to the kitchen. Before Odell can rap his knuckles on the table, I hop up and throw my arms around his neck. "Thank you, Gramps. I know you're not going to physically be here every time I come for breakfast, but in my heart you'll always be here." Reaching out, I rap my knuckles twice on the tabletop and plant a big kiss on his scruffy cheek.

Odell's cheeks redden, and he kisses the top of my head before returning to the grill.

Erick gestures with a forkful of pancake. "Did Silas take care of that injured electrician?"

"Yeah. The Duncan-Moon Foundation is paying his bills while he works with occupational and physical therapy. He's got a good reputation. There'll be work for him when he's ready."

"Good. I felt pretty bad for the guy." He blinks back another wave of emotion. "It's been a rough couple days — for all of us."

"Well, Sheriff Too-Hot-To-Handle, I'm not exactly sure how I'm going to make it through this day. What about you?"

He shrugs. "No idea, Moon." He takes a deep breath and pours syrup over his pancakes. "I thought Bristol was joining us. What happened?"

Pressing my back into the seat, I grin wistfully. "She was a little hungover this morning. Best not to let the press know about the underage drinking at the victory party last night, Sheriff."

Erick gives a loud, "Whew. No kidding. She totally saved the day, though. It was smart of her to call Eddie and give that anonymous tip to dispatch."

A proud mama smile lifts my cheeks. "She's gonna be an excellent addition to the team. I told her to take the day off, but she said she has to post about the case."

My husband stops a bite of pancakes in midair. "She's still gonna run the blog about you?"

"Well, technically, it's about Harper and Moon Investigations, now. I told her to take full credit for this one. She deserves it."

"You're always quick on your feet. Wish I had that skill." He takes a big bite and chews thoughtfully.

"You have plenty of skills, Harper." I flash my eyebrows suggestively in case he missed my innuendo. "Also, you're a great sheriff. Have you planned your first day?"

He swallows and carefully wipes his mouth. "Not exactly. Got a mountain of paperwork . . . I did figure out where to send Paulsen, though."

"Was she in the office today?"

"No. Johnson said she cleared out before the big party last night. But I got an email from Silver Shoals this morning. Their head deputy, Saul

Rivera, is returning to New Mexico to take care of an aging parent. I'll send Paulsen up there. Effective first of next month. She's on an unpaid suspension until then."

Wiggling in my seat, I do a little seated dance of joy. "I wish you could've fired her."

He hangs his head in that "aw shucks" way. "She lost sight of things for a minute. Underneath it all, she's a good cop, Moon. She needs a fresh start. Nice little town with no interfering Mitzy Moon to get under her skin."

Letting my jaw drop like the drawbridge at Rory Bombay's castle, I lean forward. "I'm the problem?"

Erick chuckles, and his blue eyes sparkle with the joy that I've longed to see for months. "Yeah, Moon. You're always the problem. That's what I love about you."

He walks his fingers across the table and turns his palm up. I place my hand in his and reply. "Yeah. And you're always the solution, Harper. That's what I love about you."

End of Book 7

A NOTE FROM TRIXIE

Hooray for Sheriff Harper! Thank you for joining Mitzy and Erick on their new adventures in **Harper and Moon Investigations**. As always, I'll keep writing them if you keep reading . . .

The best part of "living" in Pin Cherry Harbor continues to be feedback from my early readers. Thank you to my alpha readers/cheerleaders, Angel, Scott, and Erin. HUGE thanks to my fantastic beta readers who always give me actionable and honest feedback: Veronica McIntyre and Nadine Peterse-Vrijhof. And big "small town" hugs to the world's best ARC Team – Trixie's Mystery ARC Detectives!

My wonderful editor Philip Newey provided insightful notes on some "breadcrumb" issues. Many thanks to him! I enjoy getting his feedback as

I improve each case. I'd also like to give a shout out to Roxx at Proof Perfect for the excellent proofing! Any remaining errors are my own.

Big thanks to Goose for all the slick millennial speak. I was definitely vibing with it!

FUN FACT: I've been in the crew for both television and "big screen" productions!

My favorite line from this case: Turning, I treat the head nurse to one of my most condescending gazes. ~Pyewacket

I'm currently writing book three in the **Christmas Catastrophe Mysteries** series, *Linzer Cookie Murder*. I hope you'll join us in Silver Shoals for a quick visit!

Thank you for continuing to hang out with us.

Trixie Silvertale (August 2025)

PEPPERMINT COOKIE
MURDER

When Santa's daughter leaves the North Pole on a baking quest, will her sweet dreams turn fatally sour?

Cindy Claus is excited to open her own bakery. She's determined to pursue her passion and have her holiday treats prove she's more than a Yuletide heir. But before she can whisk up a success, her roommate is murdered and Cindy is the prime suspect.

With finding the real killer the only way to beat the rap, Cindy relies on the kindness of strangers and her father's trusted arctic fox. But without a recipe for success in the unfamiliar human world, grilling the wrong suspects could put her behind bars...

Can Cindy sift out the clues before she's done and dusted?

Peppermint Cookie Murder is the first book in the festive paranormal cozy series, Christmas Catastrophe Mysteries. If you like kind-hearted heroines, furry sidekicks, and a dash of mistletoe magic, then you'll love Trixie Silvertale's tasty whodunit.

Buy *Peppermint Cookie Murder* to cook up a frenzy **today!**

*Features recipes from Cindy's bakery!

Grab your next read here!
readerlinks.com/l/5211919

Scan this QR Code with the camera on your phone. You'll be taken right to the next *Christmas Catastrophe Mysteries* adventure!

Once you're in the Club, you'll also be the first to receive

updates from Pin Cherry Harbor and access to giveaways, new release announcements, short stories, behind-the-scenes secrets, and much more!

Scan this QR Code with the camera on your phone. You'll be taken right to the page to join the Club and get your FREE Novella!

THANK YOU!

Trying out a new book is always a risk and I'm thankful that you rolled the dice with Mitzy Moon. If you loved the book, the sweetest thing you can do (*even sweeter than pin cherry pie à la mode*) is to leave a review so that other readers will take a chance on Mitzy, Erick, and the gang.

Don't feel you have to write a book report. A brief comment like, "Can't wait to read the next book in this series!" will help potential readers make their choice.

Leave a quick review HERE
https://readerlinks.com/l/4588592
★★★★★
Thank you, and I'll see you in Pin Cherry Harbor!

Heists and Poltergeists: Paranormal Cozy Mystery

Blades and Bridesmaids: Paranormal Cozy Mystery

Scones and Tombstones: Paranormal Cozy Mystery

Vandals and Yule Scandals: Paranormal Cozy Mystery

Harper and Moon Investigations

Ropes and Last Hopes: Paranormal Cozy Mystery

Bells and Bombshells: Paranormal Cozy Mystery

Rodeo Clowns and Shakedowns: Paranormal Cozy Mystery

Stiffs and Petroglyphs: Paranormal Cozy Mystery

Fatal Wines and Valentines: Paranormal Cozy Mystery

April Curses and May Hearses: Paranormal Cozy Mystery

Wheels and Dirty Deals: Paranormal Cozy Mystery

Scripts and Empty Crypts: Paranormal Cozy Mystery

Christmas Catastrophe Mysteries

Peppermint Cookie Murder: Paranormal Cozy Mystery

Apple Dumpling Murder: Paranormal Cozy Mystery

Linzer Cookie Murder: Paranormal Cozy Mystery

Chocolate Crinkle Cookie Murder: Paranormal Cozy Mystery

...more to come!

MAGICAL RENAISSANCE FAIRE MYSTERIES

Explore the world of Coriander the Conjurer. A fortune-telling fairy with a heart of gold!

Book 1:

All Swell That Ends Spell – A dubious festival. A fatal swim. Can this fortune-telling fairy herald the true killer?

Book 2:

Fairy Wives of Windsor – A jolly Faire. A shocking murder. Can this furtive fairy outsmart the killer?

Book 3:

Double Double Royal Trouble – When a treat-peddling witch is found dead, will this cursed faire crumble?

Join Sydney Coleman and her unruly ghosts, as they solve mysteries in a truly haunted mansion!

Book 1: **Moonlight and Mischief** – She's desperate for a fresh start, but is a mansion on sale too good to be true?

Book 2: **Moonlight and Magic** – A haunted Halloween tour seem like the perfect plan, until there's murder...

Book 3: ***Moonlight and Mayhem*** – An unwelcome visitor. A surprising past. Will her fire sale end in smoke?

ABOUT THE AUTHOR

USA TODAY Bestselling author Trixie Silvertale grew up reading an endless supply of Lilian Jackson Braun, Hardy Boys, and Nancy Drew novels. She loves the amateur sleuths in cozy mysteries and obsesses about all things paranormal. Those two passions unite in her Harper and Moon Investigations, and she's thrilled to write them and share them with you.

When she's not consumed by writing, she bakes to fuel her creative engine and pulls weeds in her herb garden to clear her head (*and sometimes she pulls out her hair, but mostly weeds*).

Greetings are welcome:
trixie@trixiesilvertale.com

BB bookbub.com/authors/trixie-silvertale

f facebook.com/TrixieSilvertale

◯ instagram.com/trixiesilvertale